S H A S T A
AND HER CUBS

The Struggle for Survival

by Lane Robson

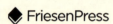

Suite 300 - 990 Fort St
Victoria, BC, Canada, V8V 3K2
www.friesenpress.com

Copyright © 2015 by Lane Robson, MD MSc FRCP(C) FRCP(Glasgow) FRSPH
First Edition — 2015

Cover Art by Patti Dyment, Canmore, AB.

All rights reserved. No part of this publication may be reproduced in any form, or by any means, electronic or mechanical, including photocopying, recording, or any information browsing, storage, or retrieval system, without permission in writing from FriesenPress.

ISBN
978-1-4602-6955-8 (Hardcover)
978-1-4602-6956-5 (Paperback)
978-1-4602-6957-2 (eBook)

1. Nature, Animals, Bears

Distributed to the trade by The Ingram Book Company

Beginnings are Important

She could feel one of the cubs snuggling towards her. They were ready to suckle and navigated based on smell rather than sight. They were only a few days old and their eyes were still closed.

At first, Shasta wondered how to tell them apart. In the darkness of her den, she needed to see without her eyes. Which cub was awake and moving towards her breast? Now she knew. Kodiak was her big boy cub, and he had a firm and assertive latch. She shifted her body to allow him to suckle more directly, and a moment later adjusted her body again when she felt the softer pull of his sister, Koda. Mato, the smallest of the three, was the last to latch.

Shasta could hardly believe how small they were now compared to how big they would become. They were so tiny, like chipmunks, and without any hair or teeth.

The den was cozy but without any light. The darkness would have been ominous in any other circumstance. During the long winter, the only light had been from an air hole, which at the surface was smaller than a squirrel. The snow that ringed the air hole was yellow from their exhaled breath. The snow cover was thick, which provided insulation.

Now that spring had arrived, much of the snow that had covered the entrance had melted away and a diffuse light filtered through thinner layers of the snow, especially when the rays of the sun found their way through the forest canopy and shone directly on the den. The snow-covered roof of the den had occasional bright pinpoints of light where the rays of sun focused through tiny ice crystals. Looking up, Shasta likened the pinpoints to stars in the night sky.

Shasta smiled as she considered her choice of such a good den in which to give birth to her first cubs. She had watched her own mother and had learned to choose a location with an entrance that faced towards the cold winter winds and away from the midday sun. This choice ensured that her den remained snow covered and invisible for longer into the spring, giving her cubs as much time to grow in safety as possible. She chose a hillside covered by a stand of evergreen trees that provided some shelter from the wind, but did not prevent the necessary accumulation of snow. The steepness of the slope under the forest canopy allowed melting water to run off without any accumulation in or around the den, but was not so steep as to restrict a heavy buildup of winter snow over the entrance. Shasta had spent a trouble-free winter.

Beginnings were important, and this one was good.

First Kodiak, and then Koda, disengaged from her breasts and rolled over into an immediate, deep sleep. She nestled them together into the fur on the inside of her upper thigh. The ground was too cold for tiny cubs and until their pelage came in, she needed to interpose her body between the cubs and floor of the den. Mato had fallen asleep while suckling. He never fed for as long as his siblings. Shasta gently moved him away from her breast. Because he was smaller, he would need the protection of his siblings, and she nuzzled him into a comfy place between them.

For the first month or so, the cubs mostly suckled and slept. Between feedings, Shasta otherwise attended to the routine cub care. Several times a day, she gave each cub a bath. Shasta repositioned one at a time to the palm of her paw. She used her tongue to gently wash the tiny naked body. Then, she repositioned the cub into her chest fur and moved another one forward for cleansing.

Today, bath time happened during the afternoon, when a soft light entered into the den. Shasta had finished washing Koda, who was now snuggled into her chest fur, and she reached for Kodiak. He was already awake, and before she could reach him, he rolled onto the den floor and cried his displeasure, from either the bumpy landing or the cold floor. Kodiak was a busy infant. He moved more than both the other two together. Shasta gathered Kodiak towards her head and his crying stopped as soon as she snuggled him against her facial fur. He fell back asleep during the tongue washing. Afterwards, she washed Mato and then nestled them together inside the downy fur of her chest.

Just before she drifted off to sleep, she thought back to the day of their birth. This had been her first pregnancy, and although happy and excited, she also felt a sense of unease. Would everything be okay? She had awakened to the sensation of wetness between her thighs and the cubs delivered at dawn, the start of a new day, which felt correct for the start of new lives.

She had wondered how many cubs she would deliver. She knew most bears had two, but she had hoped for three. Shasta could not think of any reason why she should not have three cubs. She was strong and healthy, and she was especially fit and fat when she entered the den. The father, Ursus, was the strongest grizzly in the region. Three cubs seemed only right with all these advantages. Shasta wanted three cubs because this would almost guarantee that some would survive. Mountain life was harsh, especially at the extremes of age.

Three cubs emerged from her womb. They looked healthy and were active, but one was appreciably smaller. She recalled her happiness during those first few minutes, when she licked away the fluid from their bodies so they wouldn't get a chill and then nestled them against her breasts. They had suckled immediately, and each was different. Once all had latched and were suckling well, she had felt deliciously content with life.

These remembered feelings were happy and she fell into a deep sleep, just as she had on that first day.

As deep as she slept, she awakened immediately when she felt Kodiak roll away again from her chest. It was now daylight and she could see the faint outlines of Koda and Mato still nestled in the fur of her chest and that of Kodiak a little distance away, lying on his back in the evergreen boughs she had used to insulate the floor of the den. Kodiak's tiny paws were moving in the air. His legs moved as if he was running.

Shasta had dreams, and she wondered if perhaps Kodiak might be dreaming too. He seemed to be running and she tried to imagine what he might be running towards, since as yet he had so little experience of life. She wondered if she might have shared dreams with her cubs during the pregnancy. She decided that if Kodiak was running, he was likely running towards his mother. She decided to help him.

She gently rolled Kodiak back into her fur before his body temperature could fall. She shuddered to think what might have happened if she hadn't awakened or, worse yet, if this had happened to Mato. The area for a few inches around the earthen walls was too cold for a newborn cub. She didn't know how she knew this, but she did. The den was a warm and cozy place for a grizzly mother, and would also be for older cubs. But without intimate contact with Shasta's warm furry body, the cubs would not survive a single day in their birth chamber.

When she next awoke, she could hear the winds in the trees above. They were coming from over the mountain behind the den and she knew they would be warm and dry.

The winds were a perpetual mystery. Where did they come from, and where were they going? The winds must visit other bears in other valleys. This one came from the direction of the valleys were Ursus lived, and she enjoyed the thought of sharing it with him.

Warm winds and hot days meant the snow would melt soon, and they would need to leave the den. Shasta's first thought was that they would leave before the snow had completely melted away the entrance, perhaps as soon as the cubs opened their eyes. Then she decided they would wait until their eyes were open and they were strong and steady when they walked. After a thorough and thoughtful process, Shasta concluded that she had three unique cubs, and there were too many variables to consider. She realized that she could not predict the correct time, nor did she need to. When the time was right, she felt confident she would know. The cubs started to suckle again, and she fell back into contented sleep.

As the days lengthened and the sun set progressively further up the valley, the thickness of the snow that covered the entrance thinned until Shasta could see the green outlines of the trees around the den. Koda's eyes had opened several hours earlier, and this event was followed shortly

Beginnings are Important

after, as if in sympathy with the birth order, by the opening of Kodiak's and finally Mato's.

Her daughter's eyes were cinnamon brown and immediately full of curiosity. For several days prior to their opening, Shasta had gently licked the eyes of each cub every few hours, as if to encourage the lids to separate. Her tongue was huge, almost as long as the cubs, and heavier, but she was very gentle; she used only the tip to delicately massage the tiny eyes. With this almost constant attention, she was fortunate to witness the precise moment when Koda first saw her mother. Shasta had just finished a tongue caress and was looking to see if the lids had separated at all, when both eyes opened with a suddenness that was as special as it was startling. Koda's eyes fixed on her mother's for several glorious moments before they wandered and took in the fuzzy details of her first home. Although Koda's eyes remained open for only a few moments, to Shasta, the time seemed like forever.

With her daughter's eyes open, she redoubled her licking efforts with Kodiak and was rewarded when his lids flickered open a few hours later. His eyes were much darker brown, like those of his father. They positively danced around the den before he slipped back into infant slumber. There was a sticky substance between Mato's lids that had not been present in the eyes of his siblings. She didn't like that there was a difference, but she was reassured as soon as she looked into his beautiful eyes. When Shasta's eyes first met those of Mato, he looked up at his mother with a helpless yearning and she melted into his devoted gaze.

With their eyes open, Shasta felt impatient to leave the den. She wanted to share the world with her cubs, but she restrained her new-mother enthusiasm.

She knew that it was best to wait until they were strong enough to walk down to the valley bottom.

Kodiak and Koda had grown impressively over the last three weeks. They were now as large as a mature red squirrel. Mato had not gained as much weight. But their collective weight gain, as encouraging as it was, had come at the expense of their mother's, and this was a concern for Shasta. Her eyes were hollow and her skin hung over her sides in loose folds that spread over the floor of the den like a furry blanket. She

5

was hungry, and she felt the need to eat soon if she were to continue to nurture her cubs properly.

Shasta was concerned about Mato. The size discrepancy between him and his siblings had been a worry since birth. In the darkness of the den, she mostly only saw her cubs through her paws. Her worry increased when his growth continued to lag behind his siblings. The difference was subtle at first, but Shasta's paws knew, and she understood that beginnings are important. Growth lost at the beginning was unlikely to be caught up.

The cubs were active while they suckled, but for the first month, they had mostly slept whenever they weren't feeding. Recently though, they had started to stay awake for a little while before each feeding. The cubs had learned to support themselves on their legs and had taken their first few tentative steps. Now they walked a little, back and forth in front of their mother's tummy and chest, but the relatively confined space of the den didn't really allow for much more than stretching. Still, Shasta noted with satisfaction that their legs were steadier with each passing day.

By the time the cubs were six weeks old, they were eating more and more, and Shasta was feeling hungrier and hungrier.

Shasta woke one morning to the smell of a moose. The scent aroused hunger pangs so forceful she felt compelled to leave the den and look for food, but she wondered what to do with the cubs. She couldn't take them with her, but she didn't want to leave them, either. This dilemma kept her in the den for the entire morning, but as the sun rose and the outside air warmed, the smell grew irresistible.

She wondered how the moose had died. The most likely cause was a spring avalanche. As the snow melted, the carcass would be exposed, and the smell would waft according to the prevailing winds. If the moose were close, she might be able to eat enough to sustain her and the cubs for up to week without having to feed again.

However, she also considered alternative scenarios. What if the moose had already been found, or perhaps even killed by a male grizzly?

Approaching a carcass guarded by a male grizzly would involve considerable risk. Wolves or coyotes would be okay. Not even two wolves would be a match for a hungry mother grizzly. But a male grizzly was another matter. She could easily become another meal for such a bear.

Beginnings are Important

Male grizzlies emerged from their dens several weeks before the females, and any meat odour evident to her might also attract bears from several valleys away.

Shasta considered another, even more troubling possibility. What if a man had killed the moose? A man that would kill a moose would not shrink from killing a female bear.

Shasta was conflicted. She was hungry, but she did not want to leave her cubs. Shasta knew that meat this early in the spring was a huge nutritional bonus, and not one to be missed. But her cubs needed her protection. She visualized herself eating the moose and enjoying the meal. This wakeful dream seemed real to her stomach and increased the gnawing discomfort. Shasta understood that unless she ate well, her cubs would not get enough, and these thoughts further enhanced the empty feeling in her stomach. It ate away at her resolve and finally overpowered her instinct to stay with the cubs.

She poked her nose up to the air hole and broke through the thin snow covering that had accumulated over night. She held her nose there for several minutes while she teased out the various smells that wafted in the winds above. The smell of the moose was overpowering, but even so, she could also pick up the separate smells of some deer that must have passed close by that morning, and also the ever-present odour of the squirrels. She did not smell another bear. Neither did she smell coyote, wolf, or cougar, all of which lived in her valley.

For the last week, the cubs had been staying awake for up to an hour at a time, but they always fell asleep promptly after feeding. Directly after they next fell asleep, Shasta bundled them together as far away from the entrance as possible. She pulled over some dried evergreen boughs that had served as a floor for the den and made as warm a nest as possible. Then she started to dig out the entrance.

The den was so small she had to be careful not to step on the cubs or allow snow to fall on them. She pulled her hind legs close under her body and pushed with her head and shoulders. The snow cover was modest, and with one push, she burst out into the open under a shower of snow.

A moment later, she was standing in bright sunshine and looking out over a valley that extended for some distance in both directions. Her eyes

7

took a few moments to adjust to the light after months of mostly darkness. The sun was not yet at the high point in the sky. Across and up the valley, from where she could smell the moose, the lower regions of the sun-exposed slopes had patchy light brown areas that were free of snow.

Shasta considered that if an avalanche had killed the moose, the carcass would be on a warmer, sun-exposed slope and along the path of the snow. Shasta knew her home range well, and she knew the most likely locations.

She was thirsty and ate some snow, a lot of snow, and enjoyed the cool sensation as the solid white water slipped down her throat. She ate enough to fill her stomach and then, having satisfied her thirst, she looked around again.

Fluffy, fast moving clouds were scattered high in the sky. When a cloud moved in front of the sun, the heat disappeared and Shasta felt the chillness of the wind blowing up the valley.

She looked back towards the den and her cubs, and her heart quickened as she considered their comfort and safety. She was taking a calculated risk.

She had chosen a den with a natural sleeping area that was above the entrance. She knew this would limit the effect of any cold wind, but she also knew the cubs would need more protection. She ripped some evergreen boughs from the closest tree and used them to carefully cover the entrance.

She stood back and looked thoughtfully at her efforts, and, once satisfied, turned to walk down into the valley.

The snow under the forest canopy was thigh deep, and each step seemed an effort, especially after spending six months in the den. Before she had walked far, she realized her tracks would offer a clearly visible and scent-filled trail for any predator to follow, a direct pathway to her cubs.

These thoughts bothered her and she paused, casting an anxious glance over her shoulder, but only for a moment. Then she decisively started down the mountain, and thereafter she did not look back.

Beginnings make the bear was her new mother mantra. Shasta's dream was not merely for her cubs to survive, but for them to grow into adult bears that were even stronger and fitter than she or their father.

Beginnings are Important

She walked slowly at first to allow her legs to limber up after months of inactivity. Soon thereafter, once the snow pack permitted, she started to lumber along more quickly, and sometimes, when the ground permitted, even to run. In the meadows, she slid down some of the steeper and barren slopes, and while so doing she remembered the pleasures of sliding as a young cub.

The smell of the moose weakened whenever she entered a dense thicket of trees and freshened with each meadow. She adjusted her course accordingly, and in less than an hour, she was heading up a slope on the far side. In many places, the snow had melted into a muddy mess, which made the slope slippery and the going slow.

In some areas, the snow had melted and then frozen again, and this process had repeated until there was a thick layer of ice. Shasta tried to avoid the iced areas but her impatience led to a misstep. While walking down a steeper slope over a well-established pathway covered in fresh slow, she suddenly found herself tumbling down the trail. Her body mass was sufficient to crash through the brush and to snap several smaller tree trunks before she came to an abrupt and painful stop against an evergreen tree that would not yield to her weight. The tree shook and Shasta was showered in snow and old needles.

She didn't move for a moment while she allowed her brain to catch up with the accident and to feel out the various scrapes and bruises. She could feel a wet area on her rump where an exposed rock had sliced through her fur. Every limb had a sore area. Her head had been spared any injury.

All her injuries were minor and would heel. Shasta felt fortunate. She recognized that her impatience had come at a cost. This time, the cost was low, but this was luck. She might just as easily have broken a leg. This thought brought a sudden chill of understanding. The hair on the back of her neck felt stiff and her heart raced. The survival of her cubs depended on the presence of a healthy mother. She resolved to slow down and choose each step carefully.

Slowing down had an emotional cost. She overcompensated and the slow methodical pace that she set quickened her anxiety. She was not sure how far she would need to travel to find the moose, and she knew the

9

return journey would take almost as long. She worried for her cubs and her anxiousness was the price of a prudent pace.

The early afternoon sun was hot on her back. She was not yet old enough to have the grey grizzled hairs over her spine that characterized the older bears. Her light brown coat was thick but did not have the rich lustre of a summer coat, and the loose folds that had carpeted the floor of the den now fell like furry folds below her chest and belly. The sunshine, the clear sky, and the changes of spring invigorated her. Her senses felt enhanced, and, notwithstanding the tumble, she stepped sprightly along the trails.

As strongly as the scent of the moose had pervaded the air, it took her several hours before she seemed to close in on the smell. Fortunately the wind had remained fresh and the direction in her favor. By then, she had traveled far up the valley and across several small frozen runoff streams that coursed between the mountains that lined the valley. She felt tired now, and she was keen to find the moose and return to the cubs.

The smell of the moose was now strong and Shasta suspected it was close. Where could the carcass be? Then suddenly, as if she willed it to appear, she saw the black birds, which was the same thing as seeing the moose, since they always congregated around a dead animal.[a]

An animal trail continued beyond the glade and opened up onto a slope. She bounded into the snow-filled slope and saw the debris left over from the recent avalanche. Evergreen trees in their prime had snapped under the frozen onslaught of snow and ice, and the jagged yellow pulp shone in the sunshine. She could smell the tree juices from the open trunks. She could also smell the fresh tree boughs that littered the melting snow scene. Oddly, the torn branches still looked alive, like little trees emerging at funny angles from the snow. Notwithstanding the incidental look and smell of life in these tree branches, the overpowering image and smell on the slope was that of destruction and death.

Towards the bottom of the avalanche slope, she saw the black birds feeding at the carcass. The frozen legs of the moose extended into the air like silent sentries that guarded the exposed abdomen and chest. Even at a distance, she could smell and see that the abdomen was open. The

Beginnings are Important

carcass had likely been discovered first by coyotes, and their efforts had spread the smell.

Shasta resisted the urge to go directly to the carcass. Instead, she circled into an area that would maximize the scent of any other animals in the vicinity and waited. She stood still as she watched, listened, and smelled for signs of danger. Her worst fear was a male grizzly, which, if present, would aggressively defend the carrion.

The smell of the moose was intense but she could still tease out other, less intense smells. She knew the coyotes would still be about. Likely, they had heard or smelled her before she came onto the slope. They would have scattered into the forest to watch from secure locations. She could smell them, at least two, she thought, but they were otherwise invisible. She strained her nose for any other scents, but there were no bear smells.

She did pick up the faint scent of a cougar, and this worried her, not for herself, but for her cubs. Even worse, the odour was from the direction of the den, but it was old, perhaps even from several days before.

Satisfied the carcass was safe, she lumbered casually down the slope, snorting every few steps to send an audible signal that she was in charge, and with each snort, she also smelled for danger. With her head low and swinging from side to side, her small dark eyes seemed to take possession of the entirety of her field of vision. She knew that no forest animal short of a larger bear would consider approaching her while she maintained this confident demeanour.

As she neared the carcass, the black birds flew off to a safe distance and gathered on the snow to watch and wait. The snow around the moose was blood splattered, and tiny pieces of discarded flesh lay about. The belly had been opened first by the coyotes, in the fashion they prefer. They had taken much of the viscera, but more remained. Shasta tore off a large piece of partially frozen liver and swallowed the portion whole, her first food in seven months. The chest had been opened next, and several of the ribs had been broken to gain access to the heart and lungs.

She chose each bite carefully. She knew which organs had the most food value, and wondered why the coyotes had chosen to leave the liver, spleen, and pancreas in favour of the bowel, lungs, and heart. After gorging herself with the remaining viscera and a large section of exposed

11

muscle from a hip, she felt full and ready to return to the cubs. There was still a lot of meat left. She decided to return as soon as possible.

She buried the carcass under some snow, and urinated as she left the site, her first void in many months. She hoped the smell would linger and dissuade the coyotes or other animals from returning right away. She knew the black birds would return as soon as she turned her back, and they did.

She chose a more direct route back, almost a straight line. She slid down the slopes where possible, but mostly kept to the forested areas where the snow cover was thinnest and would impede her the least. She avoided the slippery sun-exposed sections as best as she could. She still occasionally slipped, but less so as her muscles started to remember the cadences of mountain movement that fit the various types of terrain. As the afternoon wore on, she pressed herself harder, but she continued to choose her steps carefully.

The odour of the cougar strengthened as she proceeded down into the valley. She came across the remains of a rabbit it had killed and eaten a few days ago. Only portions of the fur remained. What the cougar had left, the birds and smaller animals had picked clean.

Knowing the smell was several days old was good news, but even so, having a cougar in the same valley as her cubs was a concern. On the valley bottom, she was relieved to discover that the cougar had headed into another valley, away from her cubs, and out of the scent range of the carcass.

The trip back was slower with her full stomach. Her muscles, which heretofore had only felt stiff, now felt sore, and she struggled to climb the slope and to wade through the deeper snow in the meadows. The long winter hibernation and the need to nurse three cubs had caused her to lose a lot of weight, and while most of it was fat, some was clearly muscle, and she felt the loss. Sweat covered her skin beneath her fur coat and she felt chilly whenever she stopped or was exposed to the wind. Her thirst kept up with her sweat, and she stopped often to eat snow. As the temperature fell, water from her breath frosted the hairs around her snout and mouth. Ice clung to the hairs on her chest where her sweat had flowed and frozen. By the time she reached the forest immediately below the den, the sun had set behind the mountain and the shadows of dusk had coalesced into the darkness of night.

She had been gone for much longer than she had hoped to be, and her anxiety increased as she made the final approach to the den. She stopped just below sight of it to smell and listen. She sensed nothing bad. She walked in her own footsteps back to the entrance and was relieved to find the boughs intact. Light snow had blown onto the evergreen branches. She removed the temporary door and allowed the odour from the den to surround her. She could smell each cub separate from her own scent. She heard the cubs mewing and immediately started to lactate. Moments later, she had them cuddled, and was feeding them and warming their little bodies into hers. She fell immediately into an exhausted sleep.

The next morning, she awakened refreshed. The cubs had fed several times overnight and they also awakened with extra energy, as if the moose meat had invigorated them through her.

The cubs did not look the worse for her absence. True, they had been a bit cold when she first returned, but their baby fur, thin as it had so far come in, had offered some protection, and they had prudently remained huddled together in the nest she had built. She wondered if they had explored the den at all. If they had, they had not walked far, because the slope down to the lower level was steep for a baby bear. Had they ended up at the bottom, they would not have managed to climb back up.

She did not leave the den that day, but did so the following morning, again after feeding and nesting her cubs. The smell of the moose was still present, but not as strong. She hoped there would be one more good meal.

During the intervening day, a warm dry wind had continued to howl overhead and the middle of the days had been hot. She was not surprised to see the slopes across the valley more barren of snow. This was a positive sign, because brown slopes were good for digging. When the moose was gone, but before the new plants started to grow, Shasta would need to find roots, bulbs, and tubers to eat.

Now that she knew the most direct route to the moose, and after eating and having rested for a day, the trip was quick. She purposely arrived quietly and out of the scent range from any animal that might be nearby. The only animals she could sense were the black birds that continued to pick at the remains.

Shasta considered this a bad sign. If all the large animals had given up on the carcass, there might not be much meat left.

The legs were gone, carried off no doubt by the coyotes to gnaw upon in a more secure location. Nothing remained of the chest, abdomen, and lower body but the skin and bones. The ribs formed a bony bower over an empty chest cavity. All but the shoulders and head had been neatly cleaned of meat, and these only remained because they were still frozen in the ice.

How the moose had died was now clear to Shasta. It had been following an animal trail higher up on the mountainside. While traversing the slope, likely later in the afternoon on a hot sunny day, the sudden avalanche had captured the moose and swept the creature down the mountain. As the force of the avalanche dissipated, its head and shoulders came to rest against a glacial boulder with an antler wedged under the rock. The head was at an awkward angle to the body; the neck had likely twisted and then broke against the large rock.

The boulder was in just the right position to obscure the sun and keep the head and shoulders frozen longer than the lower body. This was fortunate for Shasta, since she had the patience and strength to dig out the remaining meat, which the coyotes did not, and she proceeded to carve out the ice and snow around the remains until the shoulder haunches and head were hers to enjoy. Full, she left enough for the birds to enjoy a few more meals. She didn't bother to cover the carcass, but she did urinate to mark her territory.

She arrived back at the den to find her cubs not only up, but also on the lower level by the entrance. All three had explored far enough to slip down from the sleeping area and had been unable to climb back up. Kodiak was still trying to negotiate the incline back to the nest and Shasta smiled as she watched her big boy cub dig his front paws into the earth, spread his hind legs to slow his downward slide, and then use all his precocious grizzly strength to simultaneously pull with the front legs and push with his hind legs. Mato was the only cub sitting. He sat among some evergreen boughs and watched his brother. Koda was nosing

Beginnings are Important

around the evergreen boughs that covered the entrance and she seemed to have almost found a way out. This thought scared Shasta.

Any number of animals would enjoy a defenceless grizzly cub. Once outside the den, the cubs would be overwhelmed by the new world and it would only be so long before a situation developed that required the presence of their mother. Perhaps they would feel the chill, or they might be hungry, or they might stumble on their unsteady legs. Alone, they would mew cries of distress to attract their mother. But other animals would hear these cries, and for the meat eaters, these noises would be an auditory beacon that would pulsate through the forest with the news that a meal was available.

At about two months, the cubs were the size of small rabbit. Large birds of prey constantly patrolled the skies, and once spotted, it would only take a moment before a cub became a meal. Any of the land-based meat eaters, even the smaller ones like the mink, badgers, or wolverines, would also take a defenseless new cub.

They were too young to know danger. Shasta knew that every future trip would be more risky until all three cubs were strong enough to travel with her.

In the days that followed, Shasta limited the length of her food foraging as much as possible. Even so, the cubs now stayed awake as much as they slept, and although they still fed only about every four hours, unless Shasta returned within an hour or two, they were invariably awake and prowling around the den.

FIRST YEAR —

Innocence

Several days later, Shasta was not surprised to find the cubs outside the den.

She had left to dig for roots and tubers in the sun exposed lower regions and on the way back she heard them before she saw them. Their noises were playful, and although this reassured Shasta, she sped up all the same.

She wondered how long they had been outside. Shasta realized that the only correct answer was longer than was best.

But their emergence from the den was also a good sign. They were eager to learn about their world. This day had to come. Shasta knew there would always be risks to be taken, compromises to be made, and balances to be achieved. She had survived her childhood and she didn't doubt that she had been as adventurous as her cubs. Her mother must have left her alone, and yet she had survived her first few months. If she survived, so could her cubs.

She wondered why she couldn't remember those first few months in the den with her mother and brother. Would her cubs remember this time?

Her first memories were not of a den or of her first few steps in the forest, but from when she was older, perhaps during the first summer.

She remembered foraging for food with her mother and brother. Still, even though she did not have any earlier memories, she didn't recollect any danger in those first few months either, and surely if there had been serious threats, the bad experience would have lingered as a prominent memory. The lack of a bad memory reassured her.

Thereafter, Shasta and her cubs spent most of every day outside the den, exploring together. Every day they journeyed further from the den and each day the muscles in their legs strengthened. The cubs seemed to have two speeds: full speed or full stop.

The forest floor was a second firmament for the cubs. They were grounded first on the body of their mother; she was the floor of their infancy. Although they were now keen to explore the forest floor, when they tired, they retreated to what they knew first and best. They climbed onto Shasta and she carried them until they had rested sufficiently to walk again.

When they returned to the den at the end of each day, the cubs were tired, but less so each evening. And grow they did. By ten weeks, they were the size of a large adult rabbit and could follow their mother all day. Shasta walked slowly so they wouldn't fall behind. Even at that, they had such tiny strides that they usually ran to keep up, and although they tired quickly, every day they ran further and faster, and took shorter rest breaks. Mato was always the last cub out of the den in the morning. He took longer to wake up and seemed to need his sleep more than the other two. Outside of the den, he always trailed behind one of his siblings. He was the first to climb up on Shasta for a restful ride and the last to disembark to the forest floor.

Koda was the largest cub. She was slightly larger than Kodiak and both were noticeably larger than Mato. Shasta knew that Koda would not stay bigger for long. By adulthood, Kodiak would be half again as big as Koda.

Koda had lighter brown fur. Her front paws had splashes of gold intermingled with the brown, features she shared with Shasta's mother. Her emerging claws were also golden and Shasta wondered if they would change to the deep copper color she remembered in her mother.

Kodiak was the image of his father. His fur was thick, dark, and luxurious. The dark brown was consistent over his entire body, but not so

First Year — Innocence

deep a tone as to suggest black. The dark brown was distinctive from a distance, even in poor light. Every forest bear would know he was the son of Ursus. Even his nails were dark brown. Contrasting color could only be seen around his snout and ears. In the full sunlight, the individual hairs seemed to shimmer with a yellowish-brown hue.

Mato's fur was the opposite of Koda. His had some brown highlights on his chest, but otherwise was a much lighter golden brown. He would likely darken with time, but for now, his fur was the color of the tall blonde stalks of dry meadow grass that covered the ground after the snow melts and before the new green shoots emerged.

Shasta decided that both Koda and Kodiak were larger than other first spring cubs that she had seen. Mato, however, was not only smaller than his siblings, he was also smaller than the usual for a cub emerging from the den. He did not gain weight as well. He fed just as often, but not for as long as the other two. Usually one cub decided to initiate feeding and the other two followed. Mato was hardly ever the cub that initiated suckling. Sometimes he fell asleep while feeding, and even though Shasta jostled him awake, he always stopped before the others. While walking in the forest, Mato routinely lingered behind. Occasionally curiosity was the reason he trailed behind, but usually he was last because he could not keep up. Shasta understood this, and she did her best to slow her pace to match Mato's, while still allowing Kodiak and Koda to forge rambunctiously ahead. Sometimes this was a tough balance. Whenever Mato fell behind and was out of sight, Shasta woofed a command for Kodiak and Koda to stay put, and she turned to retrieve him. Mato loved this attention and Shasta enjoyed the giving. Sometimes Shasta made a game of the retrieval. She pretended to stalk Mato and then to either suddenly reveal herself or to give play chase. Mato mewed with joy with these games. He felt special for the extra attention. Often the other two cubs joined in. If Mato was really tired, Shasta lifted him onto her back for a rest while the others carried on. These games were fun, and, so long as the food was plentiful, the pace could be relaxed. Shasta hoped the spring would remain lush and bountiful.

Every day was a new wonder for the cubs, and Shasta shared their infant joy as they explored their new forest home. Shasta felt a part of the springtime, as if her life were somehow in synchrony with the season. Heretofore she had always enjoyed the evolving verdure, but only as an observer; now she felt as if she were an intimate participant. That her cubs should emerge into the forest at the same time as the buds appeared on the trees and just as the fresh shoots poked their way above the ground cover felt right to Shasta.

Not only did she experience a special sense of belonging to the land and to the season, but she also sensed the landscape differently. Colors were more vivid and smells were more vibrant. There was clarity and splendour to her surroundings that she had never before noticed.

Even areas still blanketed in winter white came alive. Tiny brilliant points of light shimmered down the slopes and the shadows from the tall trees alternated with the glistening lines of sparkling snow.

Shasta had never noticed the beauty of sun and shadow before, but she did not doubt the grandeur had been there all along for her to see. She wondered if her cubs saw the loveliness that surrounded them and realized this was unlikely, but she hoped that when they were older that they too might experience this joy.

All cubs are curious. Kodiak was usually the first to do anything. He was bold, even for a bear cub, and Shasta realized he might someday be one of the great grizzlies. Koda was cautious by nature, and planned her steps more carefully. Mato was mostly a follower, and his curiosity was commonly that of the sibling he was currently with. He enjoyed their discoveries vicariously.

Before the snow disappeared, the cubs learned to slide down the slopes. Shasta didn't need to show them. They discovered this pleasure all on their own, which is the way of bears that grow up on a snowy mountain.

Kodiak was the first to learn the slide game. The cubs had just awakened from an afternoon nap after gorging themselves on berries left over from the past autumn. The red berries that clung to the low-lying bush were sweet and intoxicating, the sugar having fermented over the warm autumn and still warmer spring months.[b] Kodiak awakened first, and, mischievous cub that he was, he prodded Koda and Mato until they were awake.

First Year — Innocence

Shasta watched their antics with maternal amusement. They had slept on a sun-exposed bluff, just within the forest, and out of sight of all but the rays of the sun that poked through the trees. They were on a mountain some distance from their winter den. An adjacent snow-covered slope beckoned to Kodiak, who bounded out of the forest and onto the snow. His front paws landed on an icy patch. He slipped forward, rolled over, and tumbled a few times until he found himself on his back, sliding down the slope, spinning in circles. He came to a gentle stop on a flattened area towards the bottom.

Shasta watched first with some trepidation, but once she realized there were no trees or boulders in his path and that the end of the slope did not cascade over into a deep ravine, she sat back and relaxed.

Koda watched at first without understanding what had happened. Her brother was with her one moment and at the bottom of the slope the next. In fact, by the time Koda looked again, Kodiak was bounding up the slope, excited as could be, and keen to go down again. He did so, and on the third trip, Koda and Mato both joined him.

Shasta let the cubs play while she scouted for berries or grassy areas that might be dug for roots or tubers. She also kept a wary eye skyward for large birds that would consider a small cub an attractive meal, and her nose peeled for predators that prowled the forest. However, food choices on the sliding slope were limited and Shasta was eventually obliged to interrupt their play so that she might continue to forage in other locations.

Life was mostly easy for the cubs. They only needed to keep up with Shasta. Whenever they were hungry or tired, she would give them a ride or stop and allow them to suckle and rest. They had no cares or concerns. They were oblivious to the myriad of potential dangers about them.

Shasta, however, did not share their innocent view of forest life. Every day, she came upon signs that forest life was harsh and anything but carefree.

Coming around the corner on a snowy trail one morning, the bears flushed out a large bird that had been standing in the snow beside the path. Shasta saw the blue-gray back, dark head, and the momentary penetrating gaze of the eyes before the raptor flew off, low to the ground and around the next bend of the trail. Shasta recognized the bird by the white

21

band above the eyes. This was one of the smaller flying predators, one that usually stayed within the forest canopy and that hunted by day. Her cubs were now big enough to be safe enough from this bird, but she knew they were not yet safe from the larger birds that circled above the trees, and of those even larger predators that circled higher in the sky.

The bird had been feeding on a small animal. In the snow around where the bird had stood, there were tiny gray pieces of fur and splatters of blood. Imprints of the large wings were evident in the snow on either side. Shasta saw that the bird had pressed the animal into the ground with its claws, and steadied its body with its wings outstretched and pressed into the snow, as it tore away pieces of the animal with its hooked beak.

The cubs had looked and sniffed the spot carefully.

Shasta wondered what they had learned and whether they might remember. Had they read the same story into the blood-spattered snow? Did they now understand why it is important to search the skies as well as the land for danger?

By the time the cubs were three months old, the snow had disappeared from the sun-exposed lower slopes and lingered only in the shaded areas. For several weeks, Shasta and her cubs had left the familiarity of the winter den behind, and instead they had occupied day dens on the sunny lower slopes, closer to the tubers, bulbs, and roots that sustained them. The cubs' milk teeth had erupted at the appropriate time and they were now able to supplement the breast milk with the food they would need to eat for the rest of their lives.

All three cubs were growing well. Mato had started to feed more. He was now gaining weight better and getting stronger by the day.

There had been ample food that spring, and the dead moose had provided a great start for the cubs, but they had not happened upon any other carcasses. Shasta knew these meat meals would be few and far between. Perhaps they might find a young deer or a migrating elk to kill, but otherwise they would need to satisfy their hunger by foraging for plant food.

The roots and tubers of a taller plant with hanging droplets of creamy yellow flowers was one of their richest sources of food.[d] The plants were plentiful along creek banks, in moist woods, along animal trails, and up

First Year — Innocence

avalanche slopes sometimes as high as the furthest limits of the forest. Shasta taught the cubs to eat the seedpods and then to dig for the roots and tubers. This plant offered excellent nutrition, but sustaining a mother grizzly and three rapidly growing first-year cubs meant that foraging for food was a full time preoccupation. That spring, Shasta foraged day and night while the cubs were awake, and off and on while the cubs slept in a day den.

Fresh grass shoots were another favourite food, and now that the snow was gone, the shoots were everywhere. Even before the snow had cleared, the shoots had been a regular part of her diet. Shasta could smell fresh shoots under a foot of wet snow and she had excavated some good meals in the previous days and weeks.

The days lengthened as fast as the cubs grew, and by late spring Kodiak and Koda were the size of an adolescent beaver, healthy and agile, and toughened to the terrain. Mato was still decidedly smaller, but now almost as robust, and was able to keep up.

During those first few months of life, Shasta restricted their travels to the remote regions of her home range where the likelihood of meeting another bear was low. So far, her choice of a home to raise her cubs had been good.

After Shasta left her mother during her fifth summer, she traveled for many weeks until she found a valley without the scent of another bear. She made it her first home, but the next spring she had been chased off by an older, cantankerous, and much larger female grizzly.

Shasta had stood her ground at first, but she quickly understood she was no match for the other bear. Female grizzlies continue to grow until their ninth year. Her adversary was full-grown, and the difference in size was substantial. As well, the older female was clearly an experienced fighter. She had a scar across her eye and cheek, and another on her flank. The eye beneath the scar was cloudy and sightless, and the scar on her flank was furless. Shasta knew the wounds were from another bear. Shasta considered which bear might have won a fight that led to a sightless eye in one combatant and decided that neither bear likely emerged without a wound. In this situation, there is no winner. A bear might survive a fight, but if the sustained injuries seriously undermine any basic ability,

23

and if the bear does not thrive as a consequence, then the injury is no less mortal and the dying is merely delayed because life is foreshortened. Shasta decided not to engage the older female and she moved on to find another home.

It was during that summer, when she was in her sixth year, that Shasta found the valleys that would be home to her cubs. She had traveled far before she had found the two valleys connected with a high pass. For the several weeks before she had come upon these valleys, she had not come across the scent of any bears, and her explorations did not reveal any signs of a resident bear; no scent, no droppings, no bark scratches, no diggings.

The valleys had continued to offer a safe haven. During the next two years, she had only come across two other bears, both during that first summer. One was a male, at least two years younger and smaller. The other was a much older male but unwell. Neither challenged her, and both promptly moved on without the need for encouragement.

Her home range was fortuitously unattractive to most other grizzlies. The best home ranges offered access to larger quantities of food and were fiercely competed for. Shasta's home range did not have a large river and had only average access to plant food. Much of the terrain was at higher altitude, rocky, and less suitable to support the plants favoured by grizzlies. Still, a small creek flowed throughout the year, the berry crops had been ample, and there were not so many rabbits, which meant fewer wolves and coyotes to compete with for any available meat. And it was not as if there were no deer or elk. Deer were plentiful, and higher up in the scree slopes at the end of one valley there were goats and sheep during the summer. A small herd of elk migrated through the pass that connected the valleys during mid spring. The meadows were filled with ground squirrels and the rocky outcrops were home to many marmots. All these animals were potential food. She did share the valley with families of cougar, lynx, mink, badger, wolverine, and weasel, and the cougar at least was a potential threat to her cubs, but these animals did not limit her food supply. Overall, she had chosen well.

Also importantly, she had not come across any signs of man. But she knew of men. They had periodically visited the valleys ranged by her mother. They arrived from the sky with noisy beasts that stirred

First Year — Innocence

up the earth when they landed. They killed from a distance. The few times that men had arrived, her mother had taken Shasta and her brother many valleys away to hide until the smell and sound of man had long disappeared.

By mid-spring, when her cubs were almost four months old, Shasta had relocated the family to the valley bottom. The ice and snow had disappeared from the creek and they spent their days meandering up one side and down the other while they sampled the plants that had emerged from the lush silt soil. The sand bars in the middle of the creek were one of her favourite spots to dig. Along the shoreline, the cubs ate or played with the grasses with the silky plumes that looked like the tail of the fox and moved to the rhythm of the wind.[e] The cubs enjoyed the tender tips of these plants, which they nipped off with their tiny teeth.

There were small minnows in the creek that caught the attention of the cubs, but they were much too small to offer any benefit beyond amusement. Kodiak loved to chase the tiny fish from one pool to another, and more than once Shasta had to follow her son into the water when he jumped into a pool deeper than his height. The creek never flowed fast, but Shasta knew a cub could drown even in still waters, so until they were older and had learned to swim, she would always need to be on her guard.

The rescue Kodiak routine was always the same. He would bound into a pool after a minnow and emerge sputtering and whining for help. His distress call would hasten Shasta to his rescue. She would run to his side, gather his head gently in her jaws, and relocate her soggy cub to the shore. Together they would shake away the water from their fur and, for a few hours at least, Kodiak would stick to the shoreline.

Neither Koda nor Mato ventured into deep water until they had mastered swimming in the shallow areas. Koda was the first to accomplish this and her brothers learned by watching her. Shasta was amused and impressed that Koda taught the other cubs. The water in the creek was not deep enough for Shasta to swim in, so she could not teach them. Animals all learn from their mother, and in the forest, the cubs also learn from each other. There were two lakes in the upper reaches of the adjacent valley, and some day she would take her cubs to visit these deeper

25

pools of water, and the cubs could learn to swim in deeper water, perhaps the following year.

The spring temperatures were growing hot, and before the time when the days reached their longest and hottest, Shasta moved the cubs back up the slopes to the coolness of the higher elevations. They followed the retreating snow and dug up and ate the corms of the pinkish-white flowers that sprang up like a miracle within a day after the chilly white blanket of snow disappeared.[f] The flowers were just the right height for the cubs to browse. They ate them while Shasta dug up the small corms, most of which were no bigger than an acorn, but full of good nutrition.

The late spring forest was a lively and busy place; almost all the plants were in bloom, the insects were busy, birds nested, and all the forest animals mated. The carpets of green grass and moss were a vivid contrast to the memories of the winter whites and grays. Every flower was a new color and smell, and a fresh experience for the cubs. Shasta introduced them to each plant as it erupted to grace the meadows and trails. The shapes of the trees changed from skeletal, leafless stalks to become fat bushes that blossomed above them like giant, green flowers, and provided convenient shade as their fur turned sticky with daytime sweat. Shasta's fur had moulted and the sweat that covered her glistened with the hue of health. The forest floor grew so thick with bushes that they kept more and more to the established trails.

About the time that spring gives way to summer, when the daylight has peaked and the duration of sunlight starts to shorten, Shasta and her cubs were in an area that had suffered a cleansing forest fire many years ago. In the aftermath of the conflagration, some buried evergreen cones sprouted and the tiny seedlings that emerged the next spring were now majestically tall trees that reached straight to the sky, with wide wavy boughs that created a shaded and moist environment for many of the other kinds of trees that lost their leaves over the winter. Shasta and her cubs enjoyed resting and sleeping in the day dens she created in areas with this cozy forest floor.

It was the middle of a hot day, and after a successful morning browsing the flowering plants, Shasta and the cubs returned to the day den to rest and to sleep until later when the sun was not as high and hot. Shasta

First Year — Innocence

awakened from dream sleep to the pained whelps of a cub. At first, she was disoriented, and she needed a moment to establish the reality of the situation. Another whelp engendered alertness, and she recognized the call of Kodiak and the direction of the sound. She feared that a cougar had her cub.

Koda and Mato had been asleep, but were awakened by the sudden movement of their mother as she surged away from the day den. The ground vibrated and the branches splintered as Shasta pounded her way through the brush.

Shasta burst into a tiny clearing to see Kodiak rolling on the ground, flailing his front and rear paws, and scratching frantically at his face. He seemed to be wrestling with an unknown adversary. His cries were real, but there was no blood. In the same moment that Shasta assessed her son, she saw a porcupine waddling towards the closest trees. The animal had a skin that looked like a field of grass that swayed from side to side.

Now, with her understanding that quills were the source of Kodiak's pain and that there was no mortal threat to her son, she automatically turned and precisely changed direction to intercept the fleeing porcupine.

Once Shasta was in view, Kodiak changed his voice to seek her help and sympathy, but his mother leapt past him to intercept the porcupine before the animal could reach a tree and climb to the safe haven of one of the upper branches.

Koda and Mato arrived on the heels of their mother and stopped for a moment to survey the situation. Kodiak continued to whimper and claw away at the quills.

The pained cries of Kodiak did not distract Shasta. The porcupine no longer presented as a threat, but rather as an opportunity to provide food for her family. She positioned herself between the porcupine and the nearest tree. She did not take her eyes off the porcupine, and her head moved from side to side in synchrony as the animal waddled back and forth, desperate for an opportunity to flee past Shasta to the tree. With the arrival of the other two cubs, the fearful demeanour of the porcupine changed from anxious to frantic.

The porcupine and Shasta stood head to head. While on all four legs, Shasta was twice as high and she looked down on the porcupine and

27

Shasta and Her Cubs

their eyes locked. In a forest face off, the animal that blinks or moves first is often placed at a disadvantage.

Koda and Mato slowly approached the porcupine from behind. It was aware of their approach and modestly shifted position to bring the tail into a better position to swing and engage the cubs. Shasta noticed this manoeuvre. Once the cubs were close enough, the porcupine swiped the tail and connected with Koda, who immediately recoiled and started to cry and flail away at the embedded quills. Mato was behind his sister and spared any injury.

When the tail lashed out at Koda, the porcupine was momentarily distracted, and lost eye contact with Shasta. This was all the opportunity she required. She swung the back of her paw at the head of the porcupine, which she knew would move in the opposite direction to that of the tail, and she cuffed the animal off the ground and propelled it a few feet away and onto its side. Shasta closed the gap, and before the porcupine could get up, she brought forward another paw that hit the animal behind the head, which broke the neck and rendered the porcupine lifeless.

Shasta sustained a grouping of quills in her paw with both blows and she took these in her mouth, pulled them out, and spat them on the ground. She turned her attention to the cubs. Kodiak and Koda both struggled in vain to remove the barbs. Kodiak swiped at his face in a frenzied fashion with his clawed paws, and the self-inflicted claw injuries were now as serious a problem as the quill injuries. Koda adopted a different tactic. She quickly learned that every time a quill moved, she experienced a searing pain where it was inserted. She stood still and waited on her mother.

Kodiak had barbs mostly in his nose and some around his mouth. Shasta took the barbs from Kodiak's face in her mouth and pulled them out. She licked the blood away from his face. Koda had barbs in the side of her face and Shasta performed the same procedure for her.

Mato watched this with great interest. He smelled the quills on the ground, and not having really learned why his siblings cried in pain, he investigated the dead porcupine at bit too closely. Sadly, even in death, the quills continued to be a menace. Mato brushed against the animal

28

First Year — Innocence

and some barbs managed to poke him in his right haunch. He cried out in pain and Shasta performed the quill extraction procedure another time.

Once all the quills had been removed, Kodiak stamped his paws on the ground and vocalized immature growls at the dead animal. Koda cautiously watched the dead porcupine from a respectful distance. Mato licked his pained rump.

The sun poked through the trees behind the dead animal, and the quills looked like slender streams of light. The stubby black face of the creature disappeared in the shadows of the reflected light and the quills of the dead animal glowed in the sunshine.

With the cubs attended to, Shasta turned to sort out how to eat the porcupine. The fleshy underbelly was exposed, but the quills from the side of the animal presented a myriad of painful obstacles to a good meal. The quills were longer than the length of one of Shasta's claws. Shasta's solution was expeditious but not delicate. With one swipe of her claws, she opened up the abdomen from the chest to the tail, but in the process, she suffered many quill injuries, each of which she extracted and spat out onto the ground. The abdomen was now properly exposed and she and the cubs enjoyed a nutritious end to the painful experience. Discomfort, even pain, was part of forest life. Some pains are meant to teach. Shasta knew the cubs would be respectful of porcupine quills in the future. Even more, she hoped they had learned that the pain from a few quill wounds is a modest cost for the reward of a meat meal.

By the end of the day, Shasta and her cubs finished the best part of the porcupine and the smell of death attracted other animals to the site. Shasta knew that coyotes were close but they were not a threat so long as the cubs stayed close to her. She led the cubs away from the porcupine and found a convenient night den site within the scent range of the carcass. When they returned the next morning, there was little left but the skin, quills, and some bones. Other meat eaters had taken the head and limbs away to eat in a more secure location.

Meat from two animals so early in a year was good fortune. Even without meat, there were abundant non-plant sources of food to be found. Ants and their larvae were a favourite treat. Whenever they came upon a rotten log, Shasta showed the cubs how to break open the soft

29

decaying wood or how to dig into the mushy pulp of the exposed trunk to search for insects and larvae. The cubs seemed more interested in chasing the ants than eating them, but they got the gist. With big ant colonies, the cub's paws and legs would often end up covered in a moving mass of ants, which they learned to lap up with their tongues while Shasta enjoyed the larvae in the open and vacated trunk.

Their summer routine was to awaken at dawn and travel towards a new part of the valley during the cool of the morning. If they had fed well over the prior few days, Shasta always took them through the forest and along a brand new route. If they were hungry because they had not fed as well, she took them along well-established animal trails in the most direct route possible to where she thought they might find food. Once they reached a suitable day den site with good food resources, they would sleep through the heat of the day and awaken in the evening to forage again until they felt full. Then they slept until dawn.

Foraging at night required different skills than those by day. Sunlight was not necessary to find food that was easily recognized by scent or sound, but sight was still an important asset that was diminished in the dark. On nights when clouds obscured the sky, the forest seemed more dangerous, and Shasta kept the cubs together and didn't travel as far. Different predators came out at night. Cougars could certainly snatch a cub and might disappear into the trees before Shasta could react. Even one of the large meat eating birds might consider a snatch, but by now she hoped the cubs were too big for a bird to carry. Still, Shasta kept her ears open for the sounds of wing beats, and whenever she heard the hoot of one of the larger night birds, she gathered the cubs close.

Early spring moisture and hot temperatures meant good berry growth, and Shasta was pleased that the rains had been frequent and heavy in the spring, and had continued through the hot summer. She was relieved to see so many tiny flowers on the berry bushes. The flowers augured well for a lush crop of berries. She taught the cubs not to eat the flowers on the berry bushes. Better to let the flowers survive to make berries, so that later in the summer or fall they could benefit from the enhanced nutrition contained in the fruit of the plant. Every plant and animal had a time and a place in the forest. Everything was connected.

First Year — Innocence

Rain was always welcome in the spring and summer but the accompanying lightning was not. Shasta had encountered the awesome power of lightning. She had seen a tree burst into flame on a ridge and had witnessed the deaths of animals caught in the fiery aftermath of another storm. As a young cub, she had accompanied her mother to forage in the wake of a lightning-precipitated forest fire. An entire valley had been destroyed in the space of a morning. Only a following rainstorm had prevented the fire from threatening her family. They had eaten well that evening on the remains of the deer, coyote, and smaller animals that had not escaped the smoke and flames. The lesson was clear: Run from fire, but don't neglect the opportunity to feed on the misfortune of other animals.

The cubs had heard thunder in their first weeks in the den. The sounds of spring thunderstorms were muffled, but still commanding. Within the dark confines of the den, the light from a flash of lightning sometimes seemed brighter even than sunlight.

Thunderstorms are always a worry for bears in a den. During late autumn of her second year as a cub, Shasta's family had been driven from her mother's well-chosen den by a large male grizzly. The season was well advanced and her mother was forced to accept a less optimal location and had less time to prepare the new site. The new den was not located on a steep enough slope, and the sleeping area had not been dug out high enough from the entrance. During a heavy spring thunderstorm, the den had flooded and forced them to leave. Had that happened the prior year, during her first few months of life, she and her brother would not have survived the cold exposure. Thunderstorms can kill with cold just as surely as with heat.

One especially hot morning in late summer found Shasta and her cubs working their way back towards a grassy saddle between two mountains. They had followed the emerging berry crops from the lower elevations back up the valley. The predominant flower along the trails at that time was a yellow flower that sat atop a stalk at just the right height for the cubs to enjoy as they meandered along with their mother.[8] When a breeze blew, the flowers waved as if to purposely capture their attention. Mato relished the moving flowers more than the still ones, and they became a

31

Shasta and Her Cubs

game. Sometimes he stood in front of the blowing plants and snapped at the flowers as they passed his mouth. Other times he ran at them from the trail and tried to eat them on the run.

By the time they reached the grassy saddle, the heat of the day had peaked and the cool breeze on the exposed plateau was refreshing. From this vantage point, Shasta could see through to other mountains and valleys she had never explored.

Shasta sat on top of a mound, which was a high point in the middle of the plateau, and watched her cubs alternately graze the grasses and flowers and play with each other.

The cubs loved to run after each other and the variations of the chase game were many. The chase usually ended with one cub catching the other, and they wrestled, tumbling together in the grasses until something else caught their attention. Other times they chased insects, small animals, or birds. These games usually ended in a friendly tussle, since, when the butterfly or whatever else they chased got away, they turned to each other to vent their energy.

Shasta felt comfortable and relaxed, which was an uncommon experience so far during her motherhood. She had a clear view of her cubs and they were happy and playful. They had fed well since leaving the den. The day was sunny and warm. Yes, she thought, so far the motherhood experience had gone well. She luxuriated in her feelings, the warmth of the day, and the activities of her cubs.

After the cubs were comfortable walking on four legs, they started to experiment walking on their two hind legs. Surprisingly, Mato, while weaker than his siblings, achieved this first. Walking on two legs seemed to come naturally to him and he made use of this talent to the bother of his siblings. For the days that he alone could walk on two legs, he did so at every opportunity, proud to display a talent not yet shared with his siblings. Koda learned next and finally Kodiak. Shasta was happy for Mato, who was more often the last to learn any new skill. The happy look on his young face as he literally danced his two-legged way around his siblings was as pleasurable to his mother as it was frustrating to Kodiak, who had little experience with humility.

32

First Year — Innocence

The cubs were content to play and Shasta was content to watch. A boulder just bigger than the size of the cubs proved an attractive prop for a new game that Koda discovered. The cubs were rarely out of one another's sight, and when one did disappear, the other two inevitably went looking. Koda waited until Kodiak and Mato were preoccupied with a grasshopper, and then she hid behind the rock. Grasshoppers rub their legs together when they fly, and this makes a distinctive sound. Once Koda heard that sound disappear in the distance, she knew that the grasshopper chase was over, and that Kodiak and Mato would look around for her. They did and were surprised to discover that she was not in view. The plateau was expansive but relatively flat and treeless. Kodiak saw his mother, but Koda was nowhere to be seen. Shasta had seen Koda hide and was content to sit on the mound and watch the evolving game. Kodiak and Mato ran to their mother as if Koda would somehow be with her, but the sister was still nowhere to be seen. They sniffed the air but they had already played for some time on the plateau, and Koda's scent seemed everywhere at once and nowhere in particular. They kept their nose to the ground and tried to follow the paths she had taken, one of which eventually led to the boulder. Koda had waited patiently and as soon as Kodiak passed, she tackled him from behind. Mato joined the tussle, and the cubs wrestled playfully, happy to have discovered a new game. Kodiak, however, didn't seem to understand the strategy quite as well as his sister. When Kodiak hid, he would leave his rear haunch and hind legs sticking out. For Kodiak, when he couldn't see his sister, she could not see him.

Later, while still sitting and content with so many pleasant images and sensations, her reverie was interrupted by a strange repetitive click, a sound she had never heard before.

Immediately alert, she stood up and looked all around, but saw and smelled nothing. She sat back down but the clicking returned. She stood again. The clicking lasted a few moments and again disappeared, and this pattern continued, on again, off again, without any explanation. The click seemed to come out of nowhere, and each time from a slightly different direction, but mostly from where the plateau descended on the other side of the mountain.

The plateau fell off very steeply on that side of the mountain. Shasta was looking in this direction when two black birds floated across her field of vision. The birds glided on the winds that rose up the steep rise to the plateau. Shasta watched while the birds made giant lazy circles. The birds were totally black with shaggy feathers at their throat. Their rounded wings and wedge-shaped tails made for a distinctive silhouette against the sky.[h]

Shasta knew these birds well. They were the larger, but similar in shape and color to birds that had flown off from the moose carcass. These or the other black birds were often the first to find an animal that had died in an accident or of natural causes. They were so bold that they chased the large meat-eating birds that commanded the skies, and whenever Shasta heard them make their deep guttural craww-craww calls in a repetitive and almost frantic fashion, she knew the black birds had found one of those birds to harass. Today though, they didn't make any calls.

Shasta wondered if somehow the black birds had made the clicking sound. She watched them circle above, content to follow the updrafts that formed on the side of the plateau. As they glided high over Shasta with the wind behind them, she heard the distinctive repetitive click, but only while they passed over her head, and then the sound disappeared. Shasta studied the birds through several more circles and confirmed that the clicks were present only when the larger and older of the two birds flapped the wings. She realized the click came from a wing joint. She wondered why and could not fathom a reason, but added this sound to her fund of knowledge.

Shasta sat back down and ignored the birds.

Later that day, she saw another bird circling the plateau. This bird was very high in the sky and almost invisible. Shasta only saw it when sunlight glistened on the soaring wings as the bird turned. There was a golden shimmer to the feathers on the head and neck.[i] Thereafter, her eyes followed as the bird made concentric circles high over the plateau. Shasta understood that the bird was hunting and she immediately looked for the cubs and was reassured to see them together, resting in a little hollow. The ground squirrels in the meadows disappeared into their holes while the bird circled. Shasta understood that the ground squirrels were a

34

First Year — Innocence

conventional prey for this flying predator. Eventually the high-flying bird flew out of sight too.

Shasta led the cubs down from the meadow towards the tree line, where she chose a convenient day den for the night. Huddled together in a protected hollow, the bears spent a comfortable night. Once the sun went down, the temperature plummeted. Snow came that night, as it often does so high in the mountains, but only a dusting, and Shasta knew that it would not linger long the next day. When the snow did start to stay over the course of an entire day, she would know that winter was coming and that in addition to her regular duties, she would also need to keep a watchful eye for a potential den site.

After waking the next morning, Shasta considered whether to stay another day on the grassy meadow or to move on. The plateau was a good playground for the cubs and provided better than average food sources. At one end of the plateau, the meadow gave way to loose rocks that climbed up the mountainside. The prior night, while the cubs slept, Shasta had foraged for food. There were clouds of flying insects feeding on smaller alpine flowers on the slopes and in the meadows. Shasta knew they were an excellent food source, and she wondered if the insects might spend the daylight hours under the loose rocks that went up the mountain at one end of the plateau. The possibility of a good feast on these insects led her to stay another day on the plateau.

The cubs enjoyed playing and foraging in the meadow. They browsed the edible plants and chased the ground squirrels into their holes. The bears were not fast enough to catch a ground squirrel. These animals were, however, a great food source. Perhaps that autumn, once the squirrels had fattened up and were ready for winter hibernation, Shasta would teach the cubs how to dig out their dens. But for now, the squirrels were only a playful meadow game.

Later in the afternoon, Shasta browsed the loose rocks at the end of the meadow. Walking in these loose rocks was tricky. Sometimes they slipped under her paws. Mato accompanied her, and his unpractised steps on the scree resulted in a tumble down the slope, but fortunately only his little bear pride was hurt. Thereafter, Mato confined his activities to the meadow.

35

Shasta's rock excavations were successful. She found a treasure trove of the sleeping flying insects, and she lapped them up like honey. Koda was able to handle the scree and joined her, and together they feasted on thousands of the insects.

Meanwhile, Kodiak and Mato played chase in the meadow. They tumbled into one another and wrestled for a short time whenever one cub caught the other. Shasta periodically watched their play and was pleased to see that Mato seemed stronger lately. Kodiak was bigger, but Mato could now hold his own for a longer time while they wrestled, and this pleased Shasta. Finally, she thought, Mato seems to be catching up. It had taken the entire spring and much of the summer, but now he was getting his true grizzly legs under him.

The sun had settled lower in the sky and the oblique rays created shadows on the plateau and against the rocky slope where Shasta and Koda continued to turn over rocks to look for the flying insects. Koda saw her shadow on the rocks and she was amused when her dark double moved when she did. She stopped feeding and started to dance and play with her shadow. Shasta noted this and offered an admonishing woof for Koda to pay more attention to nutrition than the shadow.

Mato spotted a butterfly and decided to give chase. The colourful wings flitted from flower to flower and led him down the meadow and further away from Shasta. Kodiak had also seen the butterfly, but there was something caught between his claws and he needed to remove this before he could join his brother.

Shasta heard the warning cry of a ground squirrel. Almost immediately, a shadow swiftly passed across the rocks above Shasta and Koda. A moment later, Shasta heard Mato's terrified cry, and she looked up to see her little boy cub in the talons of the high-flying bird.

Her fear was immediate and her lightening response left Koda sitting in the scree with a slack jaw full of insects. Koda realized this cry meant danger and she took off after her mother.

Shasta galloped with her eyes ahead, and an urgent roar thundered from her chest with the full force of air from deep in her grizzly lungs.

Kodiak had been forced flat on the ground by the wind created by a single flap of the massive brown wings that flew only a few feet above

First Year — Innocence

him. Then, he heard Mato's cry and looked up to see his brother kicking and screaming under the huge bird.

Mato was dragged along the ground as the predator flapped the wings hard to achieve the necessary lift into full flight. The bird lifted him off the ground and then faltered and Mato's paws again touched the ground. Shasta looked up and was pleased to see that the bird struggled to gain flight. She galloped faster.

Mato did his part and he fought back. He struggled to free himself from the deadly grip. He twisted his head to look up at the creature that caused the pain. He could not see the yellow feet or the black claws that tore into his body, but he could see the profile of the head with dark brown eyes that chilled him and the waxy yellow area at the base of a sharp and curved bill. Mato twisted and contorted his body every which way to try to free himself from this flying nemesis.

Shasta looked up as the bird struggled to gain altitude. One moment Mato's paws were in the air and the next they were dragging on the ground. This pattern repeated as the bird strained to lift the cub into full flight. Seeing the bird's difficulties heartened Shasta. She poured all her strength into her legs and she gained further on the bird and Mato. There was a time as she hurdled a small boulder when all four of her massive legs were off the ground and she wished she could continue to fly rather than run.

The gap closed to within her range, and Shasta prepared for the final charge and rescue. Mato looked back with frightened eyes. His mother was so close and his eyes were pleading, but Shasta's eyes never saw his fear. Her eyes were sharply focused on a spot between the shoulders of the eagle. Shasta felt solid purchase under her hind legs and she pushed off with a mighty lunge. She flew high in the air and her trajectory felt good. She was just above the bird. While airborne and so close, her front legs reached out but pawed helplessly through the wake of wings that finally achieved the strength and rhythm necessary for full flight. The powerful wings propelled Mato just out of his mother's reach.. As the bird climbed and the gap increased, Shasta, physically and emotionally spent, slowed to a run. She was too late. Koda and then Kodiak ran past and continued the hopeless chase. Mato was lost.

The bird had heard and felt the single-minded power of the grizzly mother as the gap closed but the bird never considered dropping the cub. The prize was too great and the bird was powerful and experienced.

Mato continued to struggle helplessly. A struggling animal complicates flight, even for such a strong bird. Once the flight was established, rather than suffer the struggle, the eagle dug the talons deeper into Mato's neck. Shasta saw the struggling cease and Mato's body go limp.

Shasta understood what had happened but the cubs did not. They continued to chase until the eagle and Mato disappeared over the horizon.

Shasta slowed further to a heavy walk and then stopped when there was nothing else to see. She lowered her gaze to Kodiak and Koda, who turned to return to their mother.

Grief is a powerful emotion, but unlike fear, the survival value is modest and grizzlies, like most forest animals, do not devote much time or energy to cultivate this sense of loss.

Shasta knew how and why the eagle had selected Mato. The raptor had decided that the squirrels in the meadow were an experienced and wary bunch, and while they might not provide a good prey opportunity, one of the bear cubs, the smallest one, looked like a potential and attractive meal for the eaglets back in the nest. The large bird had kept a keen and watchful eye on the meadow for several days. The plateau was an ideal hunting ground and presented like a long landing strip with lots of room after the capture for a successful escape. The bird was patient and had watched and waited until just the right circumstance presented. This was the way of the forest, the survival of the fittest, and Mato was definitely the weakest cub. Shasta noted this and then carried on. She still had two healthy robust cubs.

The cubs did not understand. They would both have a memory of the event, and with time, they might come to understand the concept of death. For Koda, this memory might someday help protect her cubs.

The next morning, Kodiak and Koda looked for Mato, but he wasn't there to play. They could smell his presence in the day den and they tracked his scent all around but he was nowhere to be found. Shasta remained in the area of the plateau until the supply of flying insects was depleted. While they continued to use the day den proximal to the

First Year — Innocence

meadow, the cubs continued to search for Mato, mostly in the mornings when they awakened, or otherwise when they came across his scent in the meadow. Shasta realized that they did not understand that Mato was gone. She knew that missing their brother was natural and that they would eventually accept his loss. Perhaps in time, they would come to understand what happened. So long as his scent lingered, they continued to search for their little brother. Once the supply of insects ran out, Shasta relocated the cubs down the mountain, and in the absence of the scent of Mato, his brother and sister stopped looking for him.

By early autumn, the cubs were fat and sadly the stronger for not needing to share the available food with Mato. They could run quickly, but still not as quickly as their mother. They had the strength, but their little strides still limited their speed.

Kodiak was still too impulsive by far and continued to get into awkward and potentially dangerous situations that required his mother's attention.

One autumn day, Shasta and the cubs were harvesting red berries on a bluff just above the creek. The bushes extended up to a rise and while Shasta and Koda were busy culling them, Kodiak decided to explore over the bluff. Once over the rise, Kodiak came upon a rocky outcrop that commanded the entire area. The young cub could not resist the urge to climb up the rocks. There were natural steps of a sort, but his chosen route was still steep, almost vertical, and when he finally reached the top, he realized at once that climbing down would be another matter. The bottom looked far away, and by this time in his young life, he had fallen and hurt himself enough times, and from much lesser heights, to realize his peril. He started to howl for help. The wind, however, was blowing strongly above the rise and in the wrong direction to carry his voice, so neither his mother nor Koda could hear him. When no one arrived to rescue him, he panicked and howled even harder, but to no avail. In desperation, he tried to climb down feet first, and immediately tumbled onto a narrow ledge several feet below. The fall winded him so he sat back on his haunches and waited to catch his breath. The ground now was closer, but he was still a long way above the softer looking grass below the outcrop, and the rocks between looked hard, jagged, and unforgiving.

39

There would be no ledge to catch him with the next attempt. He would have to step carefully or fall and tumble against the rocks until he landed on the grass. He decided not to try and continued to howl for help.

Koda and her mother had gradually worked their way up towards the bluff. Shasta ate whole branches that were bursting with ripe berries while Koda was content to lick the over-ripe and fallen fruit off the ground or from the bushes directly into her mouth. The berries had a pebbled surface with tiny hairs, and were bright red when ripe and then changed to a darker, almost purple shade.[k] Once ripe, the berries separated easily from small yellow pedestals, and eventually fell to the ground. The hollow centers collected morning dew and rainwater, and attracted tiny insects.

Koda lapped up the berries from the ground beneath the bushes with great enjoyment, but eventually she grew bored with eating and wanted to play. She looked around for her brother who she knew would like to play, but Kodiak was nowhere to be seen. Her mother seemed engrossed eating the berries directly off the bushes and clearly didn't want to play. She decided to look for Kodiak.

Koda followed her brother's scent trail and as soon as she crested the rise, she heard Kodiak's frightened call. She raced towards the outcrop and found him still sitting on the ledge. He was relieved to see her, but more so to see her race back to bring their mother. Koda arrived back at the berry patch very excited. Her "chiia, chiia, chiia" warning noise was unmistakable. Shasta understood immediately and took off in the direction her daughter had come from so quickly that Koda was left behind, and when she arrived, Shasta was already pulling Kodiak down to the ground.

Shasta had stretched her full, two-legged height from a boulder on the ground towards Kodiak. As far and as dangerous as the distance down had been for Kodiak, he was fortunately within easy reach for his taller mother. She grabbed him by the fur on his side and with her mouth delicately but firmly clenched, she lifted him down to the ground.

Kodiak was excited. He immediately wrestled with his sister, as if to confirm that he was not only okay, but also undaunted by the experience.

Shasta worried for her son and wondered whether Kodiak would survive his childhood. She had already lost one cub. For many days after

First Year — Innocence

Mato's death, Shasta had kept the cubs close and refused to let them out of her sight or more than a few steps away. The cubs did not understand and their inherent curiosity and rambunctiousness thwarted their mother's best efforts. Eventually she allowed them their freedom and accepted the situation. They needed to make mistakes to learn. She could not protect them from life.

The days shortened and the overnight temperatures fell, and the leaves turned from green to yellow. Shasta brought the cubs to sun exposed slopes to dig for the tubers of the plants with the creamy-yellow flowers. The roots had grown fat over the lush summer. Shasta was pleased to see that the cubs seemed to understand the importance of this plant in their diet. Shasta hoped they had learned that spring and fall were the seasons for this particular plant. That was the way of the forest. Everything had a season.

The spring and summer rains had swollen their tiny creek and provided a watery boost to the plants on the sand bars, which blossomed to provide a fertile source of roots. Along the water-laden edge of the creek grew bushy plants, taller than Shasta, with umbrella-like clusters of creamy-white flowers with a pungent aroma.[1] Shasta ate some of the flowers and bit others off for the cubs.

By the time the snows fell and lingered in the lower meadows, Shasta was satisfied that her cubs had grown and developed well. They were larger than average for a first year cub entering the den, and this was positive, because all bears lose weight over the winter. The stronger and larger a bear is when it enters the den, the healthier and heavier it will be when it leaves in the spring. She had lost one cub, but the other two had not sustained any serious injuries.

On balance, Shasta had much to be pleased about. The first year was good for Kodiak and Koda. The cubs had experienced and learned a lot. Both had been exposed to and taught how to identify dozens of different varieties of plant. Shasta had taught them which plants were best to eat.

The cubs also learned which plants to ignore. Some caused tummy upset. Kodiak was keen to try anything and seemed slower to catch on to these lessons. He often swallowed plants without tasting them, and if the plant didn't agree with him, he usually vomited everything back up within a few minutes. Koda, on the other hand, only ate what her mother did, and even so, whenever she tried something new, she always waited to see what the plant tasted like in her mouth, and spit out anything that didn't agree with her.

The cubs had also learned which terrain supported which kind of plant, and therefore what to look for when they arrived in a meadow, creek bed, avalanche slope, or forest floor. Conversely, if they knew what kind of plant they desired, they knew where to go to find it.

Water always meant a larger variety and abundance of plants, and where the water was located determined which plants they would find. The plants that grew around groundwater within the forest were different from those that grew along the creek in the valley. Different plants grew in boggy areas located under a forest canopy compared to those that grew in bogs without as much cover. Even scree and rock-strewn areas had their own plants, albeit smaller and with less variety than at the lower elevations and closer to water.

The cubs learned the best season to harvest each plant. Grass shoots could be grazed throughout the year. Roots, tubers, bulbs, and corms were harvested in spring or autumn. During the late spring and summer, the energy of the plant was mostly in the flowers, seeds, or berries, and the roots were pulpy and less nutritious. Flowers of some plants could be eaten during the summer while others must be left to mature into berries. Shasta showed the cubs how best to harvest each plant, how to dig for each kind of tuber, how to munch off certain flowers, and which berries needed to be culled more precisely in distinction from those that could be eaten together with the leaves and branches.

The cubs learned the rhythm of growth at different altitudes and according to whether the ground was more or less sun-exposed. The tasty early spring tubers found on sun-exposed lower slopes were often still available later in the season on the less sun-exposed and higher slopes. Shasta showed the cubs how to follow the retreat of the snow and ice at the higher altitudes to look for those plants that would emerge within days of exposure to the hot afternoon sun and courtesy of the melted snow.

First Year — Innocence

Once the snow deepened in the upper meadows, Shasta returned with her cubs to the location of their first winter den. Some snow had already accumulated in the grassy hollow beneath a rocky ledge and under the stump of an exceptionally old, large, and recently dead evergreen tree. When Shasta had first come across the site, she immediately saw the natural potential for a den. The tree had started life on the rocky ledge. With time, the roots outgrew the topsoil and stretched around and over the ledge. Finally, the tree outgrew the available space and soil, and so weakened, it toppled forward and over the ledge during a big wind. The roots and the base of the trunk formed a canopy that, together with the hollow beneath the ledge, was sufficient to accommodate Shasta and her cubs. Past erosion in the hollow beneath the ledge had created two areas, a larger upper level with a rocky floor and a smaller earthen vestibule at the lower level. The heavy snowfall common to that altitude would eventually completely cover the den under several feet of snow. The slope was steep enough that runoff water would be unlikely to accumulate. The den had proven excellent for her cubs during their first winter and she hoped it would be so again for their second.

When the cubs arrived at the den site, Shasta could tell that they didn't remember the forest surroundings, but once she had excavated the snow from the entrance and they entered the den, it was equally clear that they remembered the inside and that they were happy to be home. Shasta and her cubs just fit in the den. Had Mato survived, the den would not have been big enough, but Shasta did not dwell on this thought. Instead, this seemed somehow to affirm that all was right with her family.

SECOND YEAR —

Some Experience

The den felt cramped during the second winter, but there was still enough room for the cubs to roll over and stretch a bit. They did not nurse during hibernation and relied on their fat stores.

Shasta awakened the following spring before her cubs. She was relieved to see that they looked well. They were smaller than when they entered the den, but their weight loss, relative to their size, was much less than Shasta's personal weight loss. They even had sufficient fat stores left to sustain them if the spring food opportunities were modest. Their coats looked healthy.

Shasta felt robust and keen to get out into their valley. Even so, she didn't waken the cubs. The days still seemed short and she decided to let them sleep until the spring had evolved a little more and their food choices would be better.

The winter had seemed to pass quickly, and this worried Shasta, although she did not know why.

The snow cover over the den was considerably thinner than the previous year, and notwithstanding the still short days and long nights, Shasta could tell that the outside temperature was considerably warmer than usual for so early in the spring. When she awakened one morning to a steady drip of water from the snow ceiling over the tree roots, she knew it

45

was time to leave the den. The cubs had slept restlessly for the last week, as if they too had sensed departure might be imminent.

The morning they emerged from the den was especially fine. Just before Shasta started to dig out the entrance, she heard a bird calling in one of the closer evergreen trees.

Shasta knew and liked the gray bird that made that call.[m] It was bolder than many of the other birds in the forest. These birds seemed to want to know about everything that went on beneath the evergreen trees that were their domain. Shasta had often watched these birds search for insects, seeds, and berries on the ground. A white collar separated the black head from a dark-gray back. The gray breast and forehead allowed them to disappear when they flew into an overcast sky. They were handy sentinels; their calls kept many forest inhabitants appraised that another animal was in the neighbourhood. The bird's call that morning was a chirpy hello to anyone in the vicinity.

The cubs were a year older and stronger, but this was still the beginning time of their lives, and every day needed to count somehow with food, learning, and new skills, so that they would be fully prepared when the time came for them to leave. Most cubs left in their fourth summer. Some left earlier in the third summer and a few stayed an extra year and left in the fifth summer. She would do everything in her power to insure that when they did leave, they would be ready to live on their own.

Koda needed to learn all the skills necessary to raise her own family. For Shasta, this was her reason for life and she hoped Koda would share the same spirit. She believed her daughter would. Koda was a considerate cub, gentle in her actions, protective of her brothers, and she never needed to learn a lesson twice.

Kodiak, however, would never participate in raising a family. Males didn't do that. They roamed larger ranges and were driven to mate with as many females as possible. What with roaming a large range and the yearly competition to mate, Kodiak would come into regular confrontation with other males. He would need to learn to fight to defend his range and to survive. Shasta hoped Kodiak would grow large, bigger even than his father, and that he would gain a reputation for fierceness so that all the forest animals would defer to his strength. Shasta dreamed that one day a

Second Year — Some Experience

strong and capable female bear would choose Kodiak and mate with him to produce even stronger cubs than hers.

Shasta remembered her seventh spring. She had felt ready to mate; she wanted to have cubs during her eighth spring. By then, she had roamed her home range for two years, during which she had encountered only a few male bears, and none were a potential mate.

Waiting for a male grizzly to find her didn't make sense to Shasta. This would leave too much to chance. She had seen a number of male grizzlies but she recollected only a few that seemed suitable as mates. She instinctively knew that the success of her cubs would depend not only on how well she mothered, but also on how well she chose their father.

Ursus was a majestic young grizzly, only a few years older than Shasta. His father, Ursavus, was considered the patriarch of all the grizzlies in the region. Ursavus had never lost a fight, had sired over twenty cubs, and was still robust for his twenty years. Of all the cubs he sired, Ursus was clearly the strongest and smartest, the one most likely to inherit his father's place in the grizzly order. Shasta felt Ursus would be the best mate for her, and that he would sire the strongest cubs. Perhaps their son would follow in the tradition of his father and grandfather. That had been Shasta's plan since her fifth summer when she had first seen Ursus.

That summer had been a complicated time for Shasta. She had only just left her mother, and she was searching for a suitable home range. For over a month, she had ventured into many suitable valleys only to find the area already home to larger and stronger bears. Disappointed, she kept traveling for most of the summer. One morning, she ventured into a valley so beautiful and lush with life that she realized it must surely be home to a powerful grizzly. Soon thereafter, she caught the scent of a bear. The scent was very masculine and distinctive, and she felt drawn to see the bear that commanded such a prestigious home range. Perhaps she had a premonition that this bear might eventually be her mate, although she did not yet feel ready for that, and she might have more easily ended up a meal for a larger male. But that spring had been lush, and she did not think the male would be wanting for food. That made her brave enough to follow the scent. She was careful to keep the wind in her face to ensure he would not detect her scent, and in so doing, she started to catch distant glimpses of Ursus as he foraged in his domain.

What a confident air he had; what a proud bearing. He held his head higher than most grizzlies and even from across the valley Shasta could tell that he was handsome. His fur was long, thick, and lustrous, and shone in the sunlight. Once when she watched him walk over a ridge into the sun, the hairs around his head and along the ridge of his spine seemed to glow majestically. He paused on that ridge and looked back over his shoulder directly at Shasta, or so it seemed. But he could not have seen her. She was across the valley and hidden from view within the forest edge, and the wind was in her face so he could not smell her. Even so, Shasta had a sense that she and Ursus had been introduced, and she was excited for this connection with so estimable and handsome a bear.

One morning at dawn, she watched Ursus take down a two-year-old elk. Killing an elk was not an easy task, even for a grizzly. Many bears would never do it, and if they did, success was only likely after multiple attempts.

Shasta wondered if she could take down an elk. She might need this skill, so she went over how Ursus had stalked and captured it. Every day while she watched Ursus, she learned something new and important.

His day dens were easy to find. They were filled with his scent. Usually there was a nearby tree that Ursus had rubbed and scratched. Rubbing helps to remove the winter hair to make room for the new coat. Scratching is good for the nails. His scent marked his territory. Shasta visualized Ursus rubbing the tree in the typical bear fashion. While on two legs, he rubbed his rump, then his shoulders, and finally the back of his head on the bark. Satisfied with the back rub, he turned and clawed down the tree to create a series of parallel vertical scratches down the trunk. Then he ended the ritual with a good chest rub. The scent statement was always very clear. This is Ursus' tree, and this is Ursus' territory, and while you journey here, you must respect Ursus' dominance.

Generally, she kept a healthy distance from him. The prevailing winds had been in her face since she had started to follow and as such, she was always safe from scent detection. She preferred to travel on one side of the valley and to observe him on the other. She learned to anticipate his

Second Year — Some Experience

travels according to the terrain and the availability of the food in his path. The valley was indeed lush and food was plentiful everywhere.

One day, Ursus ventured into a new valley but with the wind behind him. Shasta was torn. She wanted to continue to follow him but she was worried about her scent. If Ursus could smell her, she knew that he would stalk her. Her presence in his home range would be an affront, and finding her would be a matter of pride for him. If Ursus considered her to be of mating age, he would mate with her and she would not have much choice. She was not certain that she would be able to outrun such a virile young grizzly. If Ursus did not consider her a possible mate, he would either kill her for food or chase her off, according to his whim. Shasta prudently decided not to follow him down that valley. She left to continue searching for her own home, but from that time, Ursus was a part of her planning.

Two years later, when Shasta was in her seventh spring and ready to mate, she decided to return to the valley of Ursus, to mate with him, so that he would sire her cubs. Decisiveness and determination are good attributes for a bear, but choosing a mate and following through with it is not so simple in the forest world. Shasta knew that she would not only have to find Ursus again, but dissuade all the other male bears that she encountered before she found him.

While Shasta was reminiscing, Koda emerged from the den and immediately nuzzled her mother. The cold nose on her flank interrupted Shasta's memories and transported her back to the fine morning, the gray bird with the chirpy call, and her second year cubs.

A moment later, Kodiak burst out of one side of the den in an explosion of snow that covered his mother and sister. He heard the gray bird, ran up to its tree, tried in vain to climb, and after he fell back several times, he turned his attention to Koda, who he immediately started to wrestle. All of this was within the first minute awake after a five month sleep. His energy seemed limitless, and Shasta wondered if this was how his father was as a cub.

The day was exceptionally fine. The warmth and sunshine were welcome friends to share with muscles that needed to be stretched. They ate a lot of snow to replenish the fluids lost during hibernation. The rush of liquid energy invigorated them further.

Shasta's body did feel fine, and she could see that the cubs felt equally happy and content. Even so, something felt wrong for so fine a day. Repeatedly, Shasta paused to lift her nose, perk her ears, or glance about to see if there might be some danger. But no, there was nothing specifically worrisome that she could detect.

They played outside the den for most of the morning before Shasta led them down towards the valley where they would forage for food.

It was after taking the first few steps down the sun-exposed slope that Shasta realized what was wrong. The snow cover was very thin and their paw prints left only a mild impression, rather than the deep holes of the prior year. Only a modest amount of snow had fallen while they had hibernated, and the hot early spring days had almost melted the little snow that had accumulated.

Shasta knew a lack of snow meant drought was possible. Without early rain, and lots of it, the plants, and therefore the animals, in the valley could not thrive. Shasta's heart beat quicker and she felt anxious for her cubs. For the early part of that day she paced a lot and was distracted from the search for nutrition, but then she realized she had no control over whether the rains would come, or whether this would be a lush or a dry year. Once she accepted this concept, she was no longer distracted, and the search for nutrition resumed as the appropriate focus for her attention.

On the way down to the valley bottom, a cheeky red squirrel chattered at them. Shasta usually never bothered with squirrels. They usually stayed high in the trees and the little time they did spend on the ground was usually only to scamper from one tree to the next. They were not an easily accessible food source. Their nut caches, however, were, and Shasta decided the first lesson of the year would be to teach her cubs how to forage for them.

The squirrel bounded from branch to branch and unwittingly led them to the cache. Feeling safe on an evergreen branch high above the bears, the squirrel used sharp teeth to rip a cone off a bough and started to dissect it to reveal the nut inside. The tiny squirrel hands were dexterous

Second Year — Some Experience

and the bears watched while the animal raised the cone to the mouth and then twirled it around between the clawed fingers as the sharp incisors sawed though the hard and pointed bracts from the top of the cone to the bottom. The nut was the prize for all this effort and the rest of the cone fell below the tree to join a pile of similar pieces on the ground below.

The cache was easy to spot and smell. The detritus of the conifer cones formed huge reddish brown heaps over and around the cache.

Shasta started digging and the squirrel was furious but powerless to intervene. Shasta ignored the frantic chatter of the squirrel. Shasta's claws were over three inches long and extended about two inches beyond her toe pads. The claws were efficient diggers and her shoulder muscles were massive. She excavated the mound down below the frozen earth to the more malleable soil where the cache was located. Koda and Kodiak watched their mother keenly and with curiosity.

Had the spring been colder, the ground would have been frozen more solidly, and Shasta would have needed to work harder to achieve the necessary depth. As it was, she quickly located the cache. She ate a large quantity and then stepped back to allow the cubs to enjoy their share. The squirrel continued a furious chatter above the bears and was still making a lot of noise when the bears ambled away.

There was still enough snow in the less sun-exposed areas to reveal the tracks of other forest animals. Over the next few weeks while the snow remained, Shasta taught the cubs the smell associated with each track. They followed fresh tracks until the cubs could also smell and sometimes see the animal.

When they followed the tracks, they invariably came across places where the animals had voided or left scat, each as distinctive as the look or smell of the animal.

The yellow stains in the spring snow identified areas were the animals had voided. The smell of the urine varied not only by the animal, but also according to the recent food intake. Sometimes they came upon a place where a coyote had voided several times over a period of hours, usually in a well-concealed location with an excellent vantage to observe rabbits or other small animals. Other times they recognized the voided scent of the same animal in different locations where the animal had marked out its territory.

Scat was distinctive even without the benefit of smell. Rabbits left hard round wrinkled pellets in piles beneath trees in the forest. Weasels left narrow, tightly wound scat, tapered at one end, usually on a rock or some other prominent point at the crossroads of two trails, or at least in the middle of a trail. Crossroads or middle-of-the-trail locations were also common places for coyotes and wolves to leave their scat, which was fatter and composed of hair and bone fragments. The locations served as scent posts so that other animals would know who was in the area. Sometimes, the scent post served as a warning. Cougar and lynx scat were much less common; cats are more secretive and usually cover their presence with earth. Deer, elk, and moose scat was oval and deposited in tidy piles on the forest floor or along animal trails; the bigger the animal, the bigger the oval.

Deer were plentiful and commonly seen, but usually only from a distance. Deer had exceptional hearing and they bounded away, their white tails raised and flashing, long before Shasta or the cubs ever came close.

Coyotes were also common. Several families lived in the valley. They tracked, killed, and ate the rabbits, squirrels, mice, voles, and other small animals in their range. More than once, Shasta or her cubs saw a coyote running along the forest floor, passing so quickly and silently, in and out of view, that had they not happened to look at that precise time, they might not have seen the animal at all.

The growing season during the past year had been long, warm, and wet, and the roots and tubers that spring were excellent. The grass in the valley bottom was also lush, having been bathed in the early spring melt from above. However, Shasta could see that the grass higher up was staying brown, and she knew this was a concern for summer and autumn feeding.

One day, while Shasta enjoyed a personal rest break in the shade of a bush with long silver leaves, the cubs headed into the nearby brush to explore. Although the cubs were out of sight, she could hear their playful antics. They remained close and she felt reassured by the noise. Kodiak returned first and emerged from the bushes covered in burrs. In

Second Year — Some Experience

due course, Koda returned, covered in the same prickly and sticky seeds. The burrs were harmless and would take a few days to brush off naturally. Shasta wondered if the cubs understood their role in the life of the plant. Over the next few days, the cubs would carry and spread the seeds in different locations and when the soil was receptive, a new plant would grow. Shasta liked that her cubs were helping the plant. Someday, perhaps the tubers of these new plants might return the favor and provide food for her family.

The spring trails were easy to navigate and tiny gray birds also frequented the paths and sometimes followed the bears.[n] These curious little birds had no fear of bears and watched Shasta and her cubs from the lower branches of trees with broad fleshy green leaves. Sometimes the birds hung upside down, as if perhaps they needed to know what the bears might look like with their feet sticking up. They had a nondescript dark gray back and a light gray breast that was overwhelmed by a jet black head and throat that were separated by a snow white cheek and eyebrow. As Shasta and the cubs passed by, they would flit ahead to another branch and wait to follow their passage along the trail. The cubs were as curious about the birds as the tiny-feathered acrobats seemed about the bears. Then, as suddenly as they appeared, the tiny birds would disappear into the forest, leaving a cheery chick-a-dee a-dee a-dee call in their wake.

Each day dawned sunny and warm, and while Shasta was pleased to watch the cubs grow larger and stronger on the tubers and roots fattened from the prior year, she was less pleased for each day that came and went without rain. The creek was lower that year and in some places was only a trickle. Bears cannot predict the weather, but they can worry about their food, and Shasta had a growing sense of dread about drought, which would reduce their food choices during the coming summer and autumn.

Her growing unease led her to consider less conventional food sources. She knew that a small herd of elk would migrate during the spring over a pass and into the valley where they had denned. The valley on the other side was closer to the ranges of other bears and had a very different terrain. The natural entrance to her home range was at the lower end of this valley. She considered both valleys to be within her home

53

range, and for the several years before she delivered the cubs, she frequented both equally.

Shasta thought back to how Ursus had stalked and killed the two-year old elk. If Ursus could do it, then so could she. Even a yearling would be a huge food boost for them.

The journey to the pass that connected the valleys would usually take several days. However, having decided on this course of action, Shasta was impatient to reach the pass and she hurried and shortened the trip by half. She worried that perhaps she might be too late and the elk might already have come and gone.

Walking along the valley bottom or through the trees on the sun-exposed slope was easy enough, but once they came to the head of the valley, the slope was steep in sections, steeper than the cubs had yet experienced, and Shasta was relieved when they didn't lag behind. They were strong cubs. When they did tire, they climbed on her back.

There was a small fertile area complete with a meadow in the pass between the two valleys. This is where the elk would pass and where she would have the best opportunity to capture at least one of the younger, less experienced animals. She knew exactly where she would wait. If the wind were just right, anything was possible.

The final part of the journey up to the pass was above the tree line. A grassy area gave way to large rocks and boulders, which became progressively smaller until only scree remained.

Scree is dangerous for any animal. No animal is safe if the ground shifts beneath the legs. Shasta had once witnessed a goat slide down a scree slope and meet its death at the bottom of a rocky ravine. True, the goat had been older and lacked the agility of younger years, but if that could happen to a goat, then that could surely happen to her, or to one of her cubs.

She was gruff with her cubs while they walked up the scree. She was frightened that Kodiak might get rambunctious or otherwise fool around, and make a mistake. There were yellow butterflies about and she worried he might decide to give chase. For Shasta, butterflies were no longer innocent creatures. She would never forget that a butterfly had lured Mato away and out of his mother's protective reach.

Second Year — Some Experience

While on the scree, whenever Kodiak or Koda strayed even a few feet from her side, she gave them a gruff and decisive come-close woof, and they understood and did just that. She purposely kept them just above and beside her, in case they slipped.

There was a natural path through the scree, and they kept to this route. It would be the same path the elk would take, and Shasta was pleased to note that there were no fresh signs of elk: no droppings, nothing to suggest they had missed the migration.

They reached the meadow between the valleys and the cubs wanted to stay and play, but Shasta kept them moving through the pass and into the next valley. She wouldn't even let them stop to relieve themselves. She didn't want their scent to linger. She knew the elk would rest and feed in this meadow, perhaps even spend the night, depending on when they arrived, and she didn't want anything to raise their suspicion.

There was always a lot that could not be predicted. No matter how smart an animal, there were always surprises that had not been anticipated. Even so, Shasta felt confident that if Ursus could take down an elk during a lush year and only for himself, then she could do this during a lean year for her cubs.

Shasta and the cubs established a day den that was further down the valley, too far away to convey a scent, even if the wind changed. They foraged and they waited.

The elk didn't arrive for many days, by which time all traces of bear scent had disappeared in the pass. The elk arrived at dusk and decided to sleep in the meadow. The wind continued to blow from the pass and Shasta smelled the elk soon after their arrival.

She decided not to take the cubs. Much as she would have liked them to watch and learn, the first priority was to obtain food. Next year they could learn how to stalk and bring down an elk, or perhaps even later this year with a young or sickly deer or moose if the opportunity presented.

She decided to attack in the hour before dawn. When she woke up to leave, both cubs also awakened and wanted to follow. They tried several times to accompany their mother until she finally became gruff. Neither cub understood. Mother always took them. What was different?

55

However, while they might not have understood, they did finally obey, and Shasta left for the pass alone.

Leaving the cubs was a calculated risk. The day den Shasta had chosen would not be in the path of any elk that ran from the pass, and as long as the cubs stayed put, they would be safe from this threat. They were still vulnerable to a larger predator such as a cougar or another bear, but she had not smelled any sign of these animals.

Sounds carry at night, and Shasta knew that elk had especially acute hearing. She was glad that there was a brisk wind blowing into her face, which would muffle both her scent and the sounds of her approach.

She reached the bluff and paused before she moved up and into view. She could not hear anything unusual, only the wind. The scent of the elk was strong. Shasta moved over the bluff and positioned herself behind a boulder. There was not yet any dawn light, but the night was otherwise crystal clear and the stars and a thin crescent moon cast silver light on the rocks, bushes, and trees. The shadows behind the rocks were still, but those behind the bushes and the few scattered solitary and skinny high alpine evergreen trees moved with the wind. The night was cold and there was a frosty covering on the ground. The elk were sleeping exactly where she predicted, in a natural windbreak created by a stand of shrubs, and still a fair distance away.

Shasta knew she could run fast. Likely, even if she roused the herd, she could still capture a young elk in the confusion as they stampeded away. The goal was to find a suitable-sized elk close to the edge of the sleeping animals. Shasta did not want to venture too far into the sleeping herd. Once aroused, Shasta knew she could be injured by the stampede of frenzied animals, which was another reason she'd left her cubs behind and hoped they hadn't followed.

Yes, she could run fast. Her hip and thigh muscles were enormous, and they had always had been a personal asset that set her apart from other bears. She had even outrun Ursus that spring when they mated. It was part of their courtship ritual. She thought back to that happy time. She had allowed Ursus to chase her for most of one afternoon before she deliberately slowed down and allowed him to catch up. After their

Second Year — Some Experience

glorious coupling, they had spent most of the next week together and had coupled many times. Her pair bond memories were strong and happy.

She thought back to that time. She had emerged from hibernation keen and eager to start her seventh spring. She had lived securely in the same home range for two winters. She was ready to mate, physically, biologically, and emotionally. She had chosen Ursus and once she decided the time was right, she immediately set out to find him. She wanted to mate in late spring or early summer and she knew that it might take a long time to find him. She also wanted to wait long enough before mating to ensure that the spring food supplies would be excellent because there was no sense mating if she would not gain good weight that spring. Even though fertilized in the spring or summer, her eggs would not implant until late in the autumn, around the time of denning, and only then if she had stored more than enough food reserves to carry a successful pregnancy.

The spring food that year had been favourable, and she had happened upon several wolf kills during her journey to find Ursus. She came upon the deer and elk carcasses fairly soon after they had been felled by the wolves. The wolves had tried to chase her away, but she snapped at them and held her ground and enjoyed her fill. The wolves reluctantly accepted her presence and respectfully bided their time to eat the leftovers. The meat had been a bonus to her food reserves and had augured well for a successful pregnancy.

To reach Ursus, Shasta was forced to pass through the ranges of other bears, and each male that sensed her presence courted her. They were a motley bunch of suitors compared to Ursus, mostly older, all less virile, and none as handsome.

Shasta, on the other hand, was an attractive potential mate. She was at exactly the right age, a picture of health, and to a male grizzly, a vision of beauty.

She avoided several males by circuitous routes and by keeping the wind in her favour, but she could not avoid them all. The males who did court her all tried in vain. Some courted with gentle affections, but all resorted to force when they realized that their suit had been rejected. Shasta never felt physically compromised or threatened, and her fleet young legs never let her down. Some of the males had come close, and one had been persistent enough to maintain the chase for most of a day.

While still reminiscing about Ursus, Shasta heard a bull elk stir and she wondered if the animal had sensed her. Shasta thought not. The elk stretched and then lay back down, seemingly oblivious to any danger. His huge antlers looked formidable. Shasta did not want to run into them. It would be unlikely for a bear to die from an antler injury, but the wound could interfere with her ability to provide for her cubs, and if Koda and Kodiak didn't survive, then what was the point?

Choosing the right elk was important. Ursus chose a two-year-old with antlers that were hardly a threat, and Shasta decided that a young elk suited her as well.

The dawn would be upon them shortly and Shasta started her stalk. She waited until the bull elk was surely asleep and then moved out from behind the boulder and towards the herd.

The wind was chilly and blowing hard through the pass, enough to push the hair around her eyes back, and also enough to muffle her steps as she slowly walked toward the herd.

It was too easy. The first elk she came upon was a two-year old. An adult, presumably the mother, was nearby. Beyond, Shasta could count many sleeping animals. She looked around and spotted a second small elk, perhaps a three-year old. If everything goes well, perhaps she might kill two.

Nothing was astir. She dug in her hind paws and ran full tilt towards the sleeping elk. She was upon the first elk in a few seconds and by the time the herd awakened and had started to scatter, she had dispatched the sleeping animal with a neck blow and she turned her attention to the three-year old. The second young elk had awakened and was clearly frightened, but other similarly anxious animals hampered an escape. Before the elk could find a clear space to run, Shasta lunged over the body and brought her clawed paws down on the elk shoulders. The elk's legs buckled under her weight. Shasta bit the skinny neck of the animal and when the elk stopped moving, she stood up to look for a third prey. But for an adult with a huge set of antlers, she might have managed to

Second Year — Some Experience

bring down a third young elk, but the sharp points that loomed between her and the now mostly scattered herd dissuaded her from being greedy.

Shasta looked up at the adult elk. The moonlight glistened off the velvet that covered the network of antlers that rose like a thorny crown from the head of the elk. The elk raised its head, as if surprised, even perhaps frightened, but then lowered the antlers in a defensive posture, and maybe, thought Shasta, as the first step to an aggressive charge. She backed off slowly, never taking her eyes off those of the elk, and after a sufficient distance developed, the elk turned and ran. Within a minute of her attack, the majority of the herd had scattered away from the shrub-lined copse and back towards the valley from where they had come. As she looked after the fleeing elk, the dawn chose that moment to break. Shasta returned to the two elk she had killed, each with a fatal neck wound, one from a clawed paw and the other from the canines in her massive grizzly jaw. Neither animal moved. Shasta was happy. She opened up the abdomen of the three year old and ate some of the liver. Yes, Shasta was very happy, she had high-value food for her cubs.

Shasta went back to the day den where she found the cubs curled up and asleep. She awakened them with a prod of her nose. Before fully awake, both cubs became agitated; they could smell the elk blood on their mother. She allowed them to lick her paws and then took them back to the meadow for their first meat meal of the year.

Shasta relocated the cubs to a new day den in the pass, which had other food choices in addition to the elk. The pass was a busy thoroughfare for many animals and the smell of the dead elk would attract predators. Even though they slept close to the carcasses and were able to protect this precious nutrition, she buried the remains after each feeding. She knew that if she minimized the scent, she might limit the number of other predators who would be attracted to the smell of death.

Several coyotes and a lone wolf arrived looking to share in this bounty, but Shasta dissuaded them with some growls and bluff charges. Smaller predators likely cautiously approached but left when they realized the bears were still around. The scent of the elk, even buried for most of the day, was strong enough to attract many predators, but for these

59

opportunists, the more overwhelming scent of the bears demanded that the other animals prudently wait their turn.

The family settled into a routine. Every morning they worked away at the elk carcasses and in the afternoons and evenings, they foraged for tubers and ate the few flowers and sparse grass shoots that grew at that dry cold altitude. Later in the day, they ate more meat. Over a few days, they ate the best parts of the two elk.

Shasta wondered if the attack would lead the elk herd to change their migration route in the future. On the one hand, that would be too bad, because the hunt had been easy. On the other hand, all that really mattered was that the elk had come when they were needed. Life in the forest was like that. Shasta decided not to dwell on this question, since life was always immediate. All of the animals and the plants lived in the moment, and while driven to survive, there would never be any guarantees.

They spent the remains of the springtime in the upper reaches of the fork of the new valley. This valley supported a different population of animals; there were more rabbits, and as a consequence more coyotes and wolves. A cougar was also about.

They foraged successfully, but as the hot days without rain continued, their sources of plant food dwindled. They could hear thunderstorms quite regularly, but they were always in the next valley or sometimes in the one past that. Shasta wondered how it was that the rain could fall so often in a distant valley, but not in hers.

By summer, the drought pattern was set. Beginnings were just as important for plants as for cubs, and the bone-dry spring had forestalled a lush summer. It was just as well they had killed the elk. Food would be hard to come by for the next few months. This would hurt all the animals in the forest. A lean spring was a problem for every animal. Lack of food emboldens an animal, thought Shasta, and the larger predators might be a threat. A pack of hungry wolves might be more aggressive than usual, and a cougar was always a formidable adversary.

Shasta looked at the parched earth and spindly plants trying to survive. She realized she would need to find alternate food sources. Ants and larvae were not dependent on rain, and for many days these foods became their staple. Shasta turned over large boulders by the creek bed

Second Year — Some Experience

to reveal the beetles and other insects that lived in these cold dark places. Koda and Kodiak enjoyed chasing the beetles, but by then, they had learned that capture-and-eat was more important than chase-and-play. They also raided one squirrel nut cache after another, but without rain, the crop of cones had been much thinner and the nuts therefore less.

Several summers before, Shasta had explored the lakes at the end of the other fork in the upper reaches of the valley. She had seen fish shimmering in the shallows and jumping in the deep. She had once watched some bears catch fish in a deep fast running river. Perhaps she could catch some fish. Even if she couldn't, the change in terrain would offer different and hopefully better food choices. She had also seen families of marmots and ground squirrels close to the lake. They would be fattening themselves for winter and if captured might compensate for the lack of berries.

The trip up the other fork of the valley to the lake was not long, but sufficient food was available on the way that they took their time and browsed the conventional locations for nutrition. They spent several days foraging from each day den, until Shasta was certain there were no further food opportunities available in the vicinity.

Both cubs continued to grow, but Koda was no longer larger than her brother. Kodiak surpassed his sister earlier in the spring. Ursus had been more than half again as big as Shasta, and Kodiak would continue to grow. If Kodiak followed after his father, he might be bigger than his mother by his fourth or fifth year. Shasta was pleased to think of this. Both cubs continued to be larger than the average for their age, a feat that gave much satisfaction to Shasta, especially considering how lean the food had been this year.

But the year wasn't over, and she still worried that without a good berry crop, they might eventually lose weight and enter the den at a disadvantage.

They reached the lakes as the summer was fading. As hot as the spring and early summer had been, the late summer and autumn were cool, but almost as dry. There had been some late summer rain, but too little and too late for the berry crop.

The first of the lakes was smaller. With the morning sun behind them, the water shimmered with many shades of green. At the edge, the shallow

61

water looked more yellow than green, as if yellow dust had fallen from the trees and settled as sparkles on the pebbled bottom. As the lake deepened, all the shades of forest green were reflected in progressively deeper tones until finally a bluish green dominated in the center. The wind that tossed the occasional surrounding spindly evergreen tree created sparse linear shadows that danced in the changing greenness.

The second lake was much larger and higher still in the valley where the trees were sparse. On one side of the lake was a sparse stand of shrubs. The upper lake was high enough that snow lingered year round by the edge of the water on the less sunny side of the lake. The air was still when they first arrived and the sun was behind them. The snow-covered slope above the water was perfectly reflected on the still surface and gave the impression that the snow sank deep into the lake.

Fish were visible in the lake and many hovered in the shallows by the shore and seemed at least potentially accessible to a paw, and there were a lot of them. Apart from their side fins that fluttered continuously, the fish seemed motionless.

Shasta sat by the side of the lake, watched the fish, and wondered how to catch them. While so doing, a shadow swooped over the ground and alerted Shasta to the presence of a large bird. Memories of Mato flashed to mind and her heart raced as she scanned the area for her cubs. Although they were now too heavy to be attractive prey to one of the large meat-eating birds, her heart thundered in her massive grizzly chest and her anxiety was palpable. Koda and Kodiak were together by the edge of the lake. Kodiak turned over a stone, and Koda chased the insects that scurried away.

The chewk-chewk-chewk call of the bird redirected Shasta's attention.° She turned her head to see the bird land on the barren, scraggly limb of an evergreen tree that had long since died to leave a gnarled and weathered white trunk close to the shoreline. This bird was much smaller than the flying predator that had taken Mato, and this alleviated her anxiety. The bird's dark brown back contrasted sharply with a white head and throat that were separated by a black line behind the eye. The bird was oblivious to the presence of the bears, a power and confidence that Shasta admired.

Second Year — Some Experience

The bird took off and soared over the lake in wide circles that were periodically interrupted by a sudden plummet towards the water. Shasta watched two such descents, one immediately after the other. Both were interrupted far above the water, and Shasta presumed the bird had seen a fish that had come and gone. Curious now, Shasta sat on her haunches and watched as the bird continued to patrol the lake. Shasta wondered how the bird could see fish beneath the surface from such a great height. While she puzzled over this question, the bird again streaked headfirst towards the lake, wings brought close to the body. Within only a few feet of the surface, the bird suddenly pulled up and entered the water talons first, and with an incredible splash that was so loud it startled the cubs.

The bird was totally under the water for a second and then emerged with a shiny wriggling fish clutched in its talons. Shasta watched as the bird simultaneously twisted the fish lengthwise under its body into a posture that reduced the wind resistance, and with several powerful wing beats flew a shallow path across the lake. The bird rippled the feathers from one shoulder to the next and continued to do so, back and forth, until the trail of water that dripped from the torso vanished. The drier feathers allowed for the optimal lift and the trajectory of the bird increased. In a few moments, the bird was high in the sky and eventually disappeared over the ridge.

Shasta wished she could catch fish as simply as the bird did. She had never caught one, but she did remember how other bears did. They had positioned themselves in the shallows and either swiped one out with a paw or trapped and transfixed a swimming fish on the bottom with a claw.

Shasta sat in the water and waited. And waited. And waited. The fish did not seem inclined to come close enough for her to swipe or trap, so she changed her strategy and relocated to the stream that coursed between the two lakes, where the water moved fast and was deep enough for fish to traverse. There were, however, no large fish that moved from the upper lake to the lower; mainly she saw smaller fish, most of them less than the length of her paw.

A fish, whether small or large, is still nutrition, and throughout that day, Shasta honed her technique sufficiently to swipe four fish out of the stream where they flopped on the shore until Koda or Kodiak managed

63

to trap the slippery things in their mouth. Kodiak was especially adept
at grabbing the squirming fish and enjoyed three of the four his mother
caught. Each day thereafter, Shasta caught at least as many fish, but she
took less time doing it.

The meadows around the lake were lusher for the water and the plant
food was good, even for the dry summer, and might have been enough to
fatten them up for the winter, but Shasta was not satisfied. She continued
to worry and turned her attention to the ground squirrels and marmots
in the area.

A gully strewn with boulders was home to a family of marmots.
During the heat of the day, the marmots lazed around on the tops of flatter
rocks, often nestled into natural depressions. The silver-gray coloring on
their back blended well with the rocks. The forehead and paws were also
silver-gray, but were interrupted with narrow black lines that gave an
appearance similar to the cracks or linear sunless depressions on a rocky
surface. But for their smell or a telltale whistle that directed attention to
their location, the marmots might not be spotted with a casual glance
from ground level, and perhaps even less so from the sky. She thought
back to how easy it must have been for the high-flying bird to spot Mato,
with his golden brown fur against the lush green of the meadow.

The marmots were wary of the bears, and whenever a bear came
close or even sometimes just looked in their direction, all that Shasta or
the cubs would see was the flash of a rusty brown rump and tail as the
marmot scurried behind or below a rock. The rump and tail hugged so
close to the surface and the movement was so brisk, that sometimes the
animal looked more like a fleeting brown shadow that disappeared into
shelter of the grey stones.

Shasta watched the marmots grow fatter as the autumn days passed.
They make ideal autumn meals, a perfect pre-hibernation boost. Over
time, they grew more complacent about the presence of the bears. At
first, they had scurried beneath ground whenever Shasta lumbered into
view. Likely, they could hear the ground shake even before they saw her.
Lately though, some had continued to sun themselves during the midday
heat even while the bears foraged nearby. The cubs had chased them

Second Year — Some Experience

mercilessly, but never came close to catching one, and these repeated failures likely enhanced a sense of security in the marmot colony.

The ground squirrels also seemed more complacent. They were much smaller than the marmots. Their burnt orange coloration on the nose, chin, belly, and legs blended well with the autumn colors in the meadows. Similar to the marmots, the ground squirrels spent their days lying around in the sun, but mostly on grass clumps close to the entrance of their den. When the bears first arrived, they disappeared promptly into their dens and only emerged when they had passed by. Of late though, curiosity seemed to overrule caution and they often stood by the entrance to their den and repeatedly called out with a sharp high-pitched *tweep*, as if to dare the bears to give chase. At first, the cubs were happy to oblige, but the squirrels were much faster and the cubs eventually gave up the game.

Shasta constantly worried about finding good nutrition, but lately she also gave thought to where she and her cubs would hibernate over the winter. The cubs were now much too big for the old den. Shasta spent part of every day considering potential den sites. She knew the formula: predominantly sunless slope that faced the colder winter winds, steep enough to minimize water accumulation, protected by a forest canopy but not such a dense canopy to limit snow accumulation, far enough away from the local animal trails, and hopefully with the benefit of a natural hollow under a rocky ledge or tree root. A thick snow cover was necessary for both insulation and security. She found lots of sites that were sunless and steep and with suitable forest cover, but none with a suitable hollow. She did identify several sites where she could excavate the earth and fashion the den according to her own needs. She kept them in mind, but continued to look for a natural and better site. She preferred the protection of an existing and more secure rocky ledge or a huge tree root system to provide at least part of the support for the roof. There was no immediate rush to make this decision, but as the days passed, this concern would grow until she identified a good site.

During the year, Shasta had managed to expose the cubs to many of the mammals that lived in the forest and while some encounters were stalked and planned, other encounters were a surprise.

65

One morning, Shasta heard Koda growl. Only Kodiak was in sight and he turned at the same time to interpret this message from his sister. For Kodiak, the growl meant concern but not panic. Shasta understood the same message. They both bolted in the direction of Koda.

Shasta arrived first to find Koda and a young mountain goat squared off on a steep slope. Koda and the goat watched each other with wary eyes. Shasta was surprised that the goat was not already running. The encounter with the Koda seemed to have immobilized the animal. The mountain goat was higher up on the slope and the two forward legs were spread a bit apart to steady the animal as it looked down on the cub. The head and neck of the goat were drawn back over the shoulders and Shasta correctly interpreted this stance. The goat was ready to run and the head of the animal was poised high in preparation for a leap. With the arrival of Shasta, Koda looked over at her mother. Shasta never took her eyes of the goat, and when Koda moved, Shasta watched as the chest of the goat rose up further and then the animal bounded high, over Koda and down the slope much faster than a bear could hope to give chase. Kodiak arrived as the goat disappeared up a rocky area that would intimidate any sensible grizzly and Shasta was pleased to note that he did not automatically give chase. However, she was disappointed that the goat was nimble enough to escape.

They did enjoy some berries that autumn, mostly those on the larger bushes or trees. The cubs were now sufficiently tall that they could stand on their hind legs and reach the lower branches to pull down the berries on their own.[p] The berries in the tree were orange red and in clusters. A flock of smaller birds with a head crest and yellow tips to the tail nonchalantly ate the berries from the same trees and at the same time as the bears.[q]

There were always some of the red berries on the low-lying ground cover.[b] The low-lying berries seemed to survive without much moisture and while these plants bore fewer berries that year, they did produce enough for a meal.

Although the cubs gathered most of their daily nutrition on their own or were offered food found by Shasta, they also continued to intermittently suckle as a supplement. Shasta's milk was thick and greasy, and she

Second Year — Some Experience

knew her cubs thrived better for suckling. Shasta also knew that suckling in the month before hibernation was somehow even more important, as if her milk had a power to fatten up her cubs even better than the berries. Always, Shasta realized that her personal nutrition needed to be excellent to provide this extra boost for her cubs.

Shasta knew the marmots and ground squirrels would eventually hibernate. Soon they would go underground to sleep the entire winter. She also knew they lived in extensive tunnel systems, the marmots in the ground below the rocks, and the ground squirrels in the dirt. Shasta studied the various entrances to the holes of the various squirrels and marmots and based on her observations and on her smell, she made her best guess about where the main winter dens might be located. She understood how much work would be involved to dig out a tunnel system and den, and she didn't want to expend any more energy than necessary.

She chose an early morning to begin her first excavation of a ground squirrel colony. The cubs attended and understood they were to guard some of the other entrances.

The autumn nights were now cold and the mornings quite chilly. Snow overnight now lingered longer and disappeared only in the maximal heat of the day. The ground squirrel families lived underground in individual dens, hopefully not too deep. They would be sleepier first thing in the morning. If she waited several more weeks, the squirrels would be totally asleep and helpless, but winter loomed, and Shasta could not wait.

When Shasta began to dig, it was as if her paws were mighty earth-moving machines. The dirt flew high and far behind her and slowly created a mound as high as her hole was deep and much higher than Shasta's four-legged height. She could smell the squirrels and their fear. Some tried to escape by alternate holes, and did. The cubs prevented only a few slower squirrels, mostly those that hesitated at the entrance, which allowed Koda or Kodiak an extra second to execute a paw swipe. Shasta dug for the better part of the dawn until she finally broke through into the first of many little subterranean caverns filled with nesting material, food stores, and usually one or sometimes two squirrels. That day, she excavated almost a dozen squirrels, all fattened for the winter.

Several times over the next week, Shasta dug out either a ground squirrel or a marmot den. Not every dig was quite as successful; sometimes most of them escaped and there were only a few animals to harvest. They scoured the area for likely dens.

Their biggest feed was courtesy of a marmot den. After removing the rocks, the den proved to be only just below the surface. So many fat marmots were slaughtered that they had enough to eat for several days.

Before autumn progressed any further, Shasta decided to take the cubs further down the mountain to look for a suitable den site. The area around the lake had been good for them. They had eaten well and did not need to expend too much energy, which is the right balance in the time before denning. Shasta doubted that they would eat so well again until spring.

On the way to the area where Shasta hoped to find a den site, she awakened one morning to the smell of a cougar. The smell was strong and Shasta realized that the cougar had been close to the day den. She had awakened once overnight and at that time, there was no smell of a cougar. The cubs continued to sleep soundly. The cougar's visit to the area was recent, and Shasta realized it might still be around. Quickly, she was standing and hyper alert.

She stood still and listened. She could hear the breathing of the cubs. There was a bit of wind in the leaves. She heard nothing else.

While still a cub, Shasta and her mother had watched across a meadow as a cougar snatched a coyote pup from right between the two parents. The cougar suddenly appeared out of the forest, had the pup clenched in the mouth, and disappeared back into the trees before the parents gave thought to chase.

With this image in mind, Shasta methodically and carefully scanned the entire area in a circle, especially the lower branches of the trees, around the day den. She saw nothing. She used her nose to identify the scent trail and concluded that the cougar had approached from lower in the forest and had passed by on the ground only a short distance away from the bears, and then had carried on up the slope to higher ground.

Shasta was reluctant to leave the cubs to explore further. The scent was much too fresh and the cougar might only be a few trees away.

Second Year — Some Experience

She awakened the cubs and they too could smell the cougar, and although they had not yet seen a big mountain cat, they could tell by Shasta's demeanour that the smell meant danger, so they were alert.

Shasta decided to take the cubs away from the area and she led them away from the cougar and in a direction that would not carry their scent, which was down the same trail the cougar had followed to pass them. She followed the dwindling scent trail until she found where the cougar had spent part of the night. Shasta sniffed out the buried scat of the cat.

Shasta continued to follow the scent trail until she reached a fork in the path. She chose the path without any scent of the cougar and carried on for the rest of the morning and put as great a distance as possible between the cat and the cubs before she allowed them to stop for food and rest. She hoped that would be the last of the cougar, but she was worried. It had come very close, and based on the size of a solitary paw print Shasta noted in some snow-moistened earth, she knew that the cat was a large adult.

Shasta understood the potential danger. The cougar knew that Shasta had two young cubs that would be slower and easy prey. It might decide to stalk the cubs and wait for an opportunity when the mother was distracted, to snatch and carry one into the trees where a mother grizzly could not follow. Shasta's heart started to pound faster as she recollected how the eagle had stalked and killed Mato.

Shasta kept the cubs close all afternoon, and by nightfall she felt safer for them, but she slept poorly that night and awakened more often than usual. She smelled carefully with every arousal for any scent of the cougar.

Her last arousal was just before dawn, and the scent of the cougar was back. Back and very strong!

In a moment she was awake and standing. The cubs had slept against her abdomen and they woke up when Shasta suddenly stood up. She huffed and snorted and the cubs knew that danger was close. They kept close to Shasta.

The sun had not yet appeared but there was some reflected light from the low-lying cloud cover. The forest was full of shadows. There was a brisk wind in the trees and this interfered with hearing. The smell of the cougar was strong and disappeared in one direction.

Shasta presumed the cougar was in that direction and still close, and that the big cat had stalked them overnight.

Cougars do not usually stalk bear cubs with a mother, and would rarely engage a bear. An adult grizzly is too formidable an adversary, but a solitary bear cub separated from its mother might be easy prey.

It was a bold cougar to stalk a mother and her cubs. Perhaps it was experienced and had stalked and killed other cubs. Shasta understood that the big cats were notoriously successful at patiently stalking and choosing the best moment to safely snatch an animal. Shasta also knew that she could neither outrun nor out stalk the cougar. If this one had decided to risk a tangle with a grizzly mother, then an encounter was inevitable.

Another possibility was that the cougar might be old or infirm, and not able to catch the customary prey. Prey was less prevalent in a drought year. Sick or weak animals are driven by extreme hunger, and although no longer at the peak of fitness, cats that are desperate enough to risk confrontation with an adult bear are still dangerous. Infirm animals are prone to mistake, but even a weakened cougar, however disadvantaged, still has claws and teeth that can maim or kill.

Again, Shasta led the cubs in the opposite direction, this time uphill. The scent continued to be strong and Shasta's fear was that the cougar might have anticipated this choice. If this was so, the cat might actually be ahead of them, and they could be walking into a trap. She kept the cubs close by her side and scanned the trees with every step. Shasta made a lot of noise as they cautiously moved through the forest. Anxious chuffs alternated with angry growls. Any forest animal within range knew that a bear was present and almost all would avoid this sound and situation, all except those few animals who were strong enough to challenge her, or those with a hunger or an infirmity sufficient to discount the risk of death.

They came to a clearing just as the sun broke over the top of a mountain and the meadow was suddenly bright.

The clearing was steeply sloped and long but not wide, and continued up the side of the mountain and was likely created by a past avalanche. There was food to be found in this clearing and Koda and Kodiak were keen to eat. Shasta would not allow them to dig or browse the plants and

Second Year — Some Experience

encouraged them to continue through the clearing and back into the forest. They were half way through the clearing when Kodiak suddenly turned when he heard a twig snap. Shasta also heard it and turned to the noise, but Kodiak's young cub's curiosity carried him one step further, and he started to run towards the noise. Shasta instinctively followed to protect Kodiak.

While she followed after Kodiak, she realized that for a moment she would be with neither cub, and once with Kodiak, she would certainly not be with Koda.

Kodiak followed the sound to a large tree and Shasta arrived on his heels.

Shasta looked up into the tree and the morning sun captured the outline of the big cat. In a flash Shasta was up on two legs. The cat was on a sturdy branch higher than she could reach. She backed up slowly with her eyes fixed on those of the cougar. Her upper limbs were poised with claws unfurled. She growled noises meant to be menacing and to intimidate. She paused when she considered the distance appropriate, dug in her hind legs, and readied herself for the cougar. She felt sure it would attempt to swipe her eyes and blind her with the first attack.

Shasta saw the cat lean back on the haunches to prepare to spring. Shasta positioned her forearms to deflect the mountain cat and protect her eyes, and perhaps to land a lucky head strike that would stun the animal.

The cougar leapt high and above Shasta and she heard a thud as its front paws landed behind her and then the sound of padded steps running up the slope.

Shasta turned in fear, with the full knowledge that she had been outmanoeuvred.

Koda saw the cougar approach. Its mouth was open and the moist teeth that glistened in the oblique rays of the morning sunshine were headed straight for Koda's neck. The four menacing teeth looked large to Koda and frightened her. She instinctively lifted her head, and the cougar's teeth found only the top of a tough grizzly skull. There was instant pain and a deep gouge over her eye, and blood poured from the wound.

71

Shasta and Her Cubs

Apart from wrestling her brothers, Koda had no fighting experience. Once the blood streamed into her eyes and compromised her vision, she panicked and froze. Then something more primal stirred within her and instilled the basic will to survive. She realized that her cub teeth were over half the size of the cougar's teeth, and every bit as sharp. Her claws were as big as the cougar's teeth and claws, and also sharp. These thoughts and her precocious grizzly spirit empowered her to fight

While the cougar repetitively tried to bite at her neck, she twisted and squirmed and managed to successfully resist every effort. Her successful struggles deflected the teeth injuries to her scalp, but did little to prevent the claws of the cougar that ripped into her shoulder and back, and the blood streamed from these cuts as well.

The cougar realized that the failure to deal a prompt killing blow and the surprising agility of the cub to squirm away meant that the momentum necessary for success had stalled. The cougar decided to try for one final neck bite and if not successful, to disengage and run.

The ground trembling thuds of Shasta's paws startled the cougar. Shasta's angry growl consumed the clearing and gave the cougar pause. As the running thumps of the mother grizzly quickly closed on the cougar, the big cat changed strategy and decided to run.

The cougar might have escaped but for Koda, who, after a lucky and desperate squirm, swiped her claws at an unprotected chest and the cougar winced. In the same instant, Koda locked her cub canines into whatever was nearest her mouth, which at that moment was a blood-covered front cougar paw. The cougar tried to run through the wounded cub, but stumbled when Koda refused to release her grizzly grip on the paw.

The cat turned to Shasta, and made last second frantic efforts to get free. Shasta arrived in a fury and, in the last moment before contact, she lifted the trailing front leg, opened the claws to their full and frightful extent, and swung the paw hard in an arc into the body of the cougar. Before the paw and the cougar collided, Shasta felt searing pain in her face as the cougar's claws tried to blind her.

The cat did not live long enough to determine if Shasta had been seriously injured. Shasta's fatal blow with the outstretched claws penetrated the chest cage of the cougar and punctured the heart. The force of

Second Year — Some Experience

Shasta's blow pushed it up and over Koda, whose jaw grip remained firm and she tumbled with the big cat to the ground. The cougar landed still on the ground and Koda landed on its abdomen, still biting the paw. The punctured heart continued to pump and for a moment, the spurts were sufficiently forceful to cover Koda in the blood of the dead animal.

Koda relaxed her jaw and the cougar paw fell limply to the ground. She stood up beside the big cat and immediately started to tremble. This graduated to a violent shake and Shasta moved to comfort her cub while she surveyed the injuries. Koda had lost a lot of blood. The wounds on the back had penetrated the shoulder muscles, and this would interfere with her mobility for some time to come. The fur was denuded in the areas of the attack and would not likely grow back. There were tooth puncture wounds about her face and head, but none in the region of the neck. Thankfully, her eyes were spared.

Kodiak arrived and immediately started to lap up the cougar blood that continued to pour out in a succession of less and less forceful spurts. He opened up the abdomen and started to eat the liver.

Shasta licked Koda's wounds until the bleeding stopped and the wounds were clean. Shasta dug up the roots of a flat-topped white flower and ground the bitter tasting roots into the mud. She applied this root and mud mixture to the largest of Koda's wounds. Once she completed this task, both Koda and Shasta joined Kodiak and ate their fill of the cougar. The cougar looked healthy and Shasta could not find anything to suggest an infirmity. Experienced and bold, she decided, but fortunately, not experienced enough.

They stayed in the area long enough to finish eating the best parts of the cougar and for Koda's wounds to close together in the first steps of healing, and then they moved on.

Looking back as they left the clearing for the last time, Shasta saw the black birds and the insects working hard to finish cleaning the bones and the skin of the cougar. Shasta felt satisfied. Koda had showed precocious survival instincts, and her efforts had not only saved herself, but had allowed Shasta to kill the cougar and to provide precious, high-energy meat for the family.

But Shasta had lost one cub and now another had suffered a significant injury. Koda would carry the legacy of her injuries for her lifetime, but she had lived and learned. This was good practice for any forest animal, no less so for a grizzly.

Autumn was fading fast and winter loomed. Snow had started to accumulate at the higher altitudes. Shasta and her cubs had excellent food reserves, and now was the time to find and build the den.

During the late summer and autumn, Shasta had explored the upper reaches of the valley for a den site, but had not found the perfect location. The only section of the home range that she was not as familiar with was the lower reaches of the valley in which they currently found themselves. She had avoided this part of the valley because the area connected directly and easily to ranges that were potentially ranged by other bears. This was the only area she had come across other bears during the four years she had now spent there. This was therefore potentially a more dangerous area, but in the absence of an optimal den site anywhere else, and given the importance of a secure hibernation site, Shasta decided to explore the lower valley before she settled on a less ideal location.

As the nights continued to lengthen and turn colder, Shasta and the cubs explored the lower reaches of the valley. They traversed the slopes on the less sun-exposed side of the valley and stopped often to crisscross areas that showed more promise. They had almost reached the lower limit of the valley and Shasta had all but given up. She felt increasingly uneasy about the possibility of encountering a bear from an adjacent range. Her uneasiness was more than maternal anxiety or instinct. A bad memory fostered her fear.

Three summers prior, when she had ventured out of the valley to find and mate with Ursus, she had almost immediately encountered an adult male grizzly that wanted to mate. Shasta was worried that bear might still be around.

There had not been any sign of a bear when she originally discovered her home range. She had not come across any scent or sign of another bear for an entire season. That was one of the major reasons why she selected her home range. It came as a rude surprise, therefore, when within a few hours of leaving her range during her mating year, that she caught the scent of a male grizzly. The scent was strong and fresh and came from the same direction she needed to travel. She was not aware of any other way to travel out of the valley. She could either wait until the bear hopefully left and was sufficiently far away, or she could follow and hope to eventually pass undetected.

She was impatient and the wind was in her favour, so she decided to carry on. However, around midday, the wind changed and carried her scent to the bear ahead. Shasta knew this meant trouble and tried to position herself at least in a higher position and with a satisfactory view of the possible approaches. Her scent was strong and the male grizzly was keen to find her. And he did.

He was an enormous grizzly for the region, bigger even than Ursus, but older and clearly not as fit. He had sired his share of cubs and he made his intentions immediately clear that he wished to sire more. Shasta needed to get past this bear, and given the terrain, to do so she would need to let him get close and then manoeuvre around him before she gave speed to her younger limbs and could run. She allowed the male to approach within only a few body lengths. They circled each other in a traditional bear meets bear ritual of introduction. Once on the side of the trail that led to Ursus, she turned and ran like she had never run before. She galloped down an animal trail that followed a dried up old creek. Branches broke, dirt flew, sod sprayed, and gravel scattered as she poured herself into her escape. The older male had a longer stride, and for a while he seemed to slowly close in on her, but he had too many years behind him to keep up for long, and eventually he lagged further and further behind. He finally stopped to nose around at a decaying log, hoping to at least find a larval lunch for his physical exertion. Shasta ran for most of the rest of the day. That episode taught Shasta that it was better never to get that close. The next male bear might not tire so easily.

It was with these anxious thoughts that she combed the slopes of the lowermost region of the same valley for a better den site.

They proved justified, because soon thereafter she caught the scent of a male bear. Fortunately, she and her cubs were not in the scent range of the other animal. She could not tell whether it was the same male that had chased her three years before, and she did not dally to find out. She might be able to outrun it, but her cubs could not.

The cubs were excited to pick up the scent of another bear. They wanted to investigate and squawked their displeasure and were reluctant to leave. Shasta made it clear that this was not an option. She herded them back up the valley with a gruffness that neither cub understood.

Shasta knew that another bear meant trouble, and she conveyed this in clear tones. The drought might have affected the other bear, and if it had not fed well, Shasta and her cubs would be considered food.

She hustled them at a gallop back up the valley. They ran for the rest of that day and Shasta hoped that they had left before the other bear had detected them, and that it would not otherwise head in their direction.

Shasta now accepted that she would need to excavate as good a den as possible in the upper reaches of the valley, and with the days getting shorter and more snow accumulating, the den was all that mattered.

She worked hard at the best of the fall back den locations over several days. The cubs were curious, but little help. She chose a site against a rock wall, but it had no tree-cover directly above, so the snow could freely fall and cover the site. Tall evergreen trees surrounded the den site. The nearest animal trail was quite a distance. There was little to attract an animal to this location. The rock wall was too steep to climb, the vegetation at this altitude sparse, and there was no water in the vicinity.

She started her excavation quite a way below the rock face, and created a tunnel up and below the rock. The ground was not all dirt. She needed to remove many rocks, some almost the size of her cubs. She fashioned a large enough area with a flat upper level and a lower entrance. She ripped some evergreen branches off the trees to provide insulation for the floor, and once they were all inside, Shasta and her cubs were satisfied with their new winter home. The snow fell heavier over the next few days and soon covered the entrance. Apart from the air hole through the snow, which eventually took on a yellowish color, there was no other sign that three bears slept there.

THIRD YEAR —

More Experience

Winter again passed too quickly, and when they emerged to a relatively snowless spring, Shasta again worried for her cubs. They had thrived notwithstanding drought during the prior year, but that did not mean they would do so again. Drought meant danger, and two years in a row can be more than doubly dangerous.

Shasta felt strong and hoped her cubs would emerge equally so. Kodiak looked fine, but she could tell that Koda's shoulder injuries were still a concern.

In the time from the cougar attack to hibernation, Koda had walked fine and mostly without pain. However, there were times when she favoured her left leg, and whenever she used her left paw to dig, she definitely had pain. Shasta had hoped the wounds would heal during hibernation, but she could tell right away that Koda's left shoulder was still not right. Her shoulder muscles were indeed stiff after she emerged from the den, but they loosened up with time, the warm spring sunshine, and movement. Shasta did not usually see much disability in the mornings, but by late afternoon on a busy day, she could tell that Koda was still weaker on the left side. Even so, there was gradual improvement and Shasta was relieved to notice that the pain with digging was less over time.

Fleshy tubers and roots would be less common in the spring following a drought year. There would be fewer flowering plants and grass shoots to eat, and the berry crop would be reduced further. They had culled out a substantial portion of the marmots and ground squirrels in the upper reaches of the valley, and Shasta didn't know if the elk would return.

The winds that spring blew mercilessly strong and dry for the first week after they emerged from the den and swept up the last vestiges of winter snow in the lower elevations. Diggings for tubers proved slim, and Shasta could tell she was losing weight. Although she could not see any weight loss on the cubs, she feared for them as well.

Shasta heard the hollow sound first, at first faint, but then louder until the entire forest boomed with the noise. The cubs perked up their ears; the sound was new. They looked to their mother for some sense of what might be the cause. She gave them a reassuring look to indicate the noise was no threat. Koda resumed her browsing through some new grass shoots but Kodiak, with courage inspired by maternal permission, immediately scampered off to investigate. Koda followed her brother and Shasta brought up the rear.

Kodiak slowed his scamper to a stalk as he closed on the location of the noise. Koda and Shasta caught up with him. The bears emerged into a clearing criss-crossed with several trees that had fallen to the ground in a windstorm. On top of one of the fallen trees was a gray-brown bird.[r] The tail feathers fanned out behind it. Prominent neck feathers collared the head. While they watched from the edge of the clearing, the bird began to slowly beat the wings back and forth. As the tempo increased the hollow sound started and grew steadily into the loud booms the bears had heard before.

Once the cause of the noise was understood, Shasta turned to leave. This was not a nutrition opportunity; she knew the bird would fly away before the bears could get much closer. Kodiak, however, did not have this experience, and he edged into the clearing to continue his stalk. With the most recent display over, the bird stared Kodiak to a brief stop and then flew up to the lower branches of a living tree. Kodiak gave chase to the base of the tree and reached up on two legs but to no avail. The bird remained nonplussed by Kodiak's jumping and barking noises, and once

Third Year — More Experience

he realized it was not accessible, he lost interest and turned away to join his mother and sister.

It was a relief when a spring snowstorm delivered several feet of snow in the valley, a heavy enough dump to lessen Shasta's thoughts about drought. The storm had dropped so much snow that only Shasta had long enough legs to walk in some of the meadows where the snow was deepest. The cubs were not yet tall enough to walk well in the deep snow, but neither were they still light enough to ride on Shasta's back. Their combined weight was now heavier than their mother. Until the snow melted, they stayed within the forest where the canopy prevented deep accumulation.

When the sun and warm temperatures emerged after the snowstorm, Shasta decided to take the cubs back into valley beyond the pass where they had captured the elk. On the second day after the storm, she took the cubs down into the valley and followed the branch of the creek that led up to the pass.

The creek and the sun were both to one side behind a line of tall evergreen trees. Fluffy snow from the large snowfalls of the last few days hung heavy on the boughs. The midday sun was hot and the snow on the sun-exposed boughs melted. The snow on the trail had been in the sun long enough to feel sticky and to slow their progress, but Shasta and the cubs were not in a rush. They had fed well in the days before the snowfall, and to Shasta the snow was a positive sign. Moisture was welcome, whether thick and white as snow, or thin and clear as water.

The day seemed almost carefree. The cubs were old enough and strong enough that Shasta wondered whether they might leave that summer. This was not a sad thought. They were almost ready, and so was Shasta. In fact, as the spring progressed, she had felt the stirrings of the desire to mate again. She had done well as a first time mother, and now she had experience and was keen to do even better with her next litter. Perhaps she might again deliver three cubs. Maybe all three might survive with the next litter.

Shasta continued to let these pleasant images occupy her thoughts, when suddenly a shadow appeared on the ground at her feet and startled her. It disappeared as suddenly as it had come.

At first Shasta presumed the fleeting shadow had been a bird that had flown between her and the sun, and her heart quickened as Mato came to mind. But she looked and listened, and didn't see any signs of a bird.

Shasta moved on, but she stopped suddenly when the shadow re-appeared, again without a perceivable cause. The cubs also stopped and heightened their alertness to match that of their mother. Shasta could not detect any strange scent. After a few moments, reassured that no danger seemed near, she continued along the trail and was soon re-immersed in the reverie of thoughts that the shadow had interrupted. Again and again though, the fleeting shadow suddenly appeared and stopped her thoughts and movement.

The sensation unsettled Shasta. Most everything that is unexplained has this quality. Something that is unexplained and that takes away the light- and life-giving sun makes the situation worse. The memory linkage of a shadow with the death of Mato further enhanced the uneasiness of the situation for Shasta.

She remained tense. Still, no danger seemed near, and they continued, but now constantly on the alert. The shadows continued to come and go in an unpredictable pattern until by chance the cause finally became clear. Shasta had paused to look up and bask her face in the sun that shone between two tall and closely aligned evergreen trees. The sun had risen almost to the tops of the trees and felt warm and good on her face. While so looking, snow from the highest most branches suddenly slipped off the boughs and fell between the trees in a cloud of snowflakes that obscured the sun. The shadow of the falling snow was like a wall that fell between the trees. Shasta exhaled a sigh of relief. No danger was present; the falling wall of snow was only something new, but safe.

Although Shasta was reassured to see all the snow after the storm, she understood that fluffy new spring snow is not the same as hard packed winter snow. In the hot days that followed, the earth and the air sucked up the wetness in only as many days as the snow took to accumulate.

The winds turned cool and dry as they reached the pass between the valleys. As they crested the ridge into the intervening meadow where Shasta had killed the elk, the force of the wind was sufficient to slow their progress. The winds that entered the lower elevation of the pass needed

Third Year — More Experience

to keep up with the higher winds that negotiated wider expanses between the mountain that sloped up and away. It accelerated in the narrower region where the bears walked, and the force was considerable. Shasta strained against it and kept the cubs in the relatively wind-free shadow of her body.

They passed by the bony remains of the elks, which lay where the animals had fallen. What meat the bears had left had long since been scavenged by smaller animals and birds, and finally polished clean by insects. Most of the bones were no longer with the remains and only the rib cage and the attached portion of the spine was present.

Shasta led the cubs into the stand of shrubs that had protected the elk from a similar, but much less intense, wind the prior spring. They allowed the shrubs to take the force of the wind while they rested and grazed the dry grass on the ground. The wind showed no signs of lessening. Instead, the force freshened during the time that they foraged and rested.

The trunks creaked and the tops of the isolated trees waved wildly in the wind. Dead branches blew free from the trees and shrubs. The cubs were anxious. Shasta shared their concern and decided to take them down into the next valley and away from the wind.

By the time she decided to move on, the wind was at its most fierce. When she walked out of the protected shrubbery the blast seemed to take her breath away. The cubs followed again in single file, each in a staggered position behind the hip that was opposite the wind. Shasta looked behind every few steps and saw that even if she were strong enough to walk faster, that the cubs were not.

At the end of the meadow, the pass went up abruptly before it descended into the next valley. The slope up and down from the ridge was covered in scree. Shasta worried about their footing in the wind, but the scree seemed to hold and the final steepness of the rise offered momentary protection.

Shasta crested the ridge at the end of the pass, the point from where they would descend out of the wind, when something hit her face and stung her eyes, which immediately started to water. She realized that earth, plant material, and even small stones were in the air and instinctively she turned her head and body away from the wind in a protective reflex. By then, the cubs had also reached the crest, and when Shasta turned, she accidentally exposed them to its full force.

Koda was closest behind her mother, and once exposed to the wind she slipped suddenly as if some unseen paw had pushed her. Kodiak was in exactly the wrong place. He had just crested the ridge when his sister fell against him. He lost his balance, tumbled off the ridge, and slipped down the scree slope.

Shasta's eyes were watering enough to interfere with her vision, but not enough to miss the images of her son as he tumbled down the rocky slope. To Shasta, it seemed as if Kodiak bounced and rolled in slow motion, and with every descent to the ground, Shasta winced as she shared his pain.

Kodiak came to an ominously silent rest against a boulder at the bottom of the slope.

Shasta wanted to immediately race down to him, but resisted this urge and instead she herded Koda back to the protection of the small stand of shrubs before she carefully descended down the path towards Kodiak.

Kodiak was alive, but injured. The fur over his hip and one of his hind legs was matted with blood. He would not or could not stand on that leg. When she picked him up by the scruff of his neck, his leg dragged along the ground and he cried with pain. She dragged him in this uncomfortable fashion back to the shrubbery where they spent a cold and uncomfortable evening. The wind settled with the sun. Koda slept well nestled into her mother, but Kodiak's sleep was fitful. Shasta also slept poorly. The matted blood worried her. Even more, she knew that Kodiak's reluctance to put pressure on the injured right hind leg was ominous.

While Kodiak slept, she licked the matted blood from his fur with her tongue until the wound was clean. The blood tasted good, but she felt bad for this feeling, because she knew that the energy she gained from the blood was at the expense of her son. After licking the wound clean, Shasta dug up some mud and roots and pressed the mud mixture against the hip wound. She chose the roots from the same plant she had selected for Koda. The dried and dirty-white flowers from the last summer waved wildly in the powerful wind, but the sturdy stalks prevailed. She

Third Year — More Experience

remembered that her mother had once used the mud and roots from this plant to help heal a wound in her own brother.

The cubs had not suckled often the prior year and even less so this year, but still often enough that Shasta had milk. That night, she fed Kodiak several times, more to sooth and relax him with this primal intimacy than for the nutrition. Just prior to one feeding, his sleep was restless and she knew he was dreaming. He moved his legs during these partial arousals and the movement of his body and especially that of his injured leg caused him to whimper in pain. She settled him against her warm, furry belly and he suckled himself back to sleep.

Shasta was frightened about what the morning would bring. She knew what happened to animals that could not walk. They either starved to death because they could not find enough food, or they were prey to the other meat-eating animals in the forest. Nature is largely indifferent to injured or infirm animals.

Shasta recollected an injured animal incident from her childhood. When she was Kodiak's age and still with her mother, they had been foraging up a sun-exposed slope towards the top of a hill. Once she reached the crest, Shasta heard the faint and plaintiff cry of a deer from a copse of trees in the valley below. She heard the cry before her mother. The tone frightened Shasta, but when her mother heard the deer, her response was positive and excited. The mother raced towards the trees with Shasta and her brother in hot pursuit. They found the young deer with a hoof stuck in a cleft among a group of small boulders. How this happened to a deer, the most nimble-footed forest animal, was a mystery. The portion of the leg against the rocks was bleeding from its struggles to escape. Perhaps the deer had been startled, and so, distracted, had jumped and landed in an unplanned and unlucky spot. While struggling to remove the leg, the effort only served to wedge it deeper. Removing the foot would now be a tricky puzzle for a calm and methodical animal, and likely impossible for a frightened and inexperienced deer.

The family of the deer had abandoned the animal, maybe only moments before when the bears started down from the bluff, or perhaps earlier, when the inexorable outcome was understood. The accident must have happened recently, because no bleeding animal could stay undiscovered for long. The larger predators would smell the blood or hear the cries and arrive promptly. Shasta and her family happened to be the first on the scene.

In the moment it took Shasta to consider the mystery of this deer, her mother broke its neck, and in the next moment, with the same paw, she opened up its belly. They ate well that day.

This memory haunted Shasta during her fretful attempts to sleep.

When Kodiak awakened the following morning, he immediately tried to stand, but his leg collapsed beneath him. Shasta's worst fears seemed realized. Still, she didn't give up hope, and over the morning, as his muscles limbered up, Kodiak was able to take some tentative steps. By late morning, he was walking, albeit with discomfort and a limp. Shasta's relief was enormous.

She watched happily over the afternoon while Kodiak's mobility improved. By nightfall, his strength seemed almost normal. However, he continued to walk with a limp. That night she licked off the roots and mud and applied a fresh mixture. Kodiak slept better.

Shasta could tell that Kodiak's right hip was sore when he woke up the next morning, but with movement and the warmth of the afternoon, the discomfort lessened over the day. Shasta felt the discomfort more than Kodiak, who never seemed to acknowledge the pain. Shasta saw the subtle clues to the presence of pain, which perhaps only a mother could see. When Kodiak stretched a muscle from the injured area, just for a moment, Shasta saw him grimace. He retracted his lips to reveal the canines. Had she been closer, likely she would have heard his adolescent voice change from the mewing whine of a first year cub to the menacing beginnings of growl. Even so, his controlled demeanour in the presence of pain was testimony to his innate grizzly toughness.

The discomfort peaked on the third day and then improved, albeit too slowly for Shasta's peace of mind. When she could still see a limp after two weeks, Shasta's concern was high. She realized that there was still pain, and that it increased over the day. She was worried and acknowledged her worst fear. She had lost one cub. Now both her remaining cubs were injured, and for Kodiak, the stronger of the remaining two, the injury might be permanent. The injury might seriously limit his chances

Third Year — More Experience

for survival and rule out any chance that he would follow in the footsteps of his father and grandfather. Then she thought again and she decided that she might have underestimated him. Perhaps he could overcome this. Her thoughts continued to vacillate but with time, hope prevailed and she accepted the situation.

The spring included a lucky find; they came upon two elk that had been caught in an avalanche. Three wolves were eating the carcasses when Shasta arrived. They did not leave. Looking around, Shasta also noted several coyotes that kept a safe distance from the wolves, in the hope they might be allowed a turn at the carcasses.

One wolf would have left as soon as a grizzly appeared on the scene. Two wolves might have needed some mild encouragement. Three wolves meant Shasta would need to be aggressive to claim this meal.

She hesitated for a moment and considered whether the cubs would be okay. Might the coyotes pose a threat while she handled the wolves? Or, once she engaged the wolves, might one of them attack a cub while she was distracted with the others? Shasta wondered if a wolf could tell that Kodiak's right hip was a bit lame, or that Koda's left shoulder was injured. If so, either might be targeted. On balance, she decided the cubs would be safe if they stayed put. But, would they?

Then she considered whether they even *should* stay put. Both Kodiak and Koda were now in their third year. Kodiak's right leg was a liability, and although both cubs were heavier than the wolves, their experience was modest. Only Koda had been bloodied in a fight for survival. She survived the cougar attack and she had acquitted herself well. Apart from the porcupine, Kodiak had yet to be bloodied by another animal.

Koda was the cautious sibling and her cougar experience was fresh in her mind. Shasta felt Koda would do well if attacked, but doubted she would attack first. Kodiak, on the other hand, seemed quite ready to approach the wolves, and notwithstanding his injury, he seemed keen to stand haunch-to-haunch with his mother.

Shasta decided this was a teaching moment; the time had come for the cubs to learn to fight for their food.

The elk and the three wolves were off to one side and at the edge of the pathway of the avalanche. Shasta and her cubs were on the other side

85

of the avalanche path, and below the wolves. The coyotes were higher up still and on the same side as the wolves. Above the avalanche path was a tree-lined ridge.

Shasta led the cubs up the side of the avalanche path by the trees that had been spared the crushing onslaught of snow. She hoped the wolves might think she was retreating from a confrontation. Once well above the wolves, Shasta led the cubs into a stand of evergreen trees, and she continued to climb to the ridge at the top of the avalanche path. They traversed the ridge on the opposite side and out of sight of the wolves and coyotes. The wind was coming from the floor of the valley, so their scent disappeared. Once on the other side of the slope, Shasta chose a course back down that was concealed in the forest until she had an unobstructed view of the elk carcasses, the three wolves, and the coyotes.

The coyotes noticed her first and yelped a warning as they scattered into the forest, down and away from the wolves. The wolves heard the warning and looked up. Their anxiety was clear. Two of the wolves were clearly intimidated by the reappearance of the grizzlies. They stepped back from the carcasses. The third wolf was not so intimidated and held the ground.

The distance between the wolves and Shasta was not far and would be closed in a short time once she chose to run. She thought the wolves would likely scatter as soon as she first moved, but she was not certain. She wondered if the more fearful twosome might stand their ground if the dominant wolf did. If so, there would be a fight.

From deep inside Shasta, a low rumble emerged, and this sound became a hum that resonated in the air of the valley. The sound was menacing and the wolves understood the malice in this noise. Suddenly, Shasta lurched forward out of the trees, and in a flash, she was bounding down the mountain with her ears back, flattened against the side of her head. The hum changed to a throaty growl, and by the time she was ready to engage the wolves, a horrible roar blasted from her open mouth.

The two wolves that seemed likely to run bolted, but the more aggressive wolf stood its ground and then, in a deft and precisely timed manoeuvre, suddenly circled around and up the slope to force Shasta to turn while galloping down the hill. This was a simple but masterful

Third Year — More Experience

strategy. The force necessary to slow and turn an adult grizzly racing at speed down a steep slope is considerable. To accomplish this gravity-defying move with the alacrity necessary to match that of the wolf was not possible. Shasta could not slow her massive body down in time, and she substantially overshot the lead wolf.

Kodiak and Koda immediately followed their mother in the attack but they slowed and stopped when they saw the lead wolf come up towards them. They watched as their mother did her best to slow and turn, but mostly they kept their eyes on the wolf.

When the two wolves that bolted heard the considerable noise engendered by an adult grizzly sow trying to slow down and turn, they turned to look back up the slope. They saw Shasta within a cascade of ice crystals as she ploughed through the snow to turn and start back up the slope.

Once Shasta completed this turn and looked up the slope, she realized she was further away from the wolf than when she first charged from the forest edge above.

Shasta looked at the lead wolf and past the animal to her cubs higher up. For a moment, the slope was still and none of the animals moved. Then the two wolves below started to slowly walk back up the slope. Shasta turned and locked eyes with one of them. The look startled the wolf, and both animals paused, but only for a moment. Then they resumed a slow purposeful climb to close the gap with Shasta.

Shasta understood the awkwardness of the situation. While her life was not threatened, this was not the case for the cubs. A full grown and experienced wolf has killed hundreds of small animals. As with most predators, a wolf practices the killing neck bite to perfection. The neck of an inexperienced cub might be an easy target for an adult wolf. Her cubs were at risk, the lead wolf was within killing range, and Shasta, running uphill, might not reach them in time.

Both Kodiak and Koda adopted aggressive postures. They leaned down the slope towards the wolf. With their full weight above their paws, they looked bigger than they were. Their normally cute and circled ears were pulled flat against their head. Their upper lips curled back to reveal canines that could easily rip into wolf flesh. Adolescent growls, snorts, and huffs alternated with foot stamps. They did not move forward,

87

but neither did they look as if they would retreat if the lead wolf came to them.

The two following wolves and the cubs had ordinary roles to play in this skirmish. The cubs only needed to stand their ground at the top of the slope and the two wolves only needed to guard the lower slope, and the real action would happen between. The cubs and the two wolves below were reserve fighters, and they waited for the battle to join. For now, this would be a battle fought by the strongest and most experienced animal warriors in the field.

The lead wolf understood that he had the advantage of three experienced forest fighters, compared to only one in Shasta. He was an alpha male, the leader of a larger pack, and he was clearly up for the fight.

A confident and aggressive solitary wolf is not so common and Shasta wondered if perhaps this one had stood ground with a bear before. If so, this was not good news for Shasta, because an experienced animal, even a smaller one, can easily inflict serious injury on a larger animal. Left only to bulk, massive strength, and endurance, a large number of wolves were no match for an adult grizzly, but only if the wolves fought one at a time. However, this is not how wolves fight, and the four adult animals on that slope all knew that once the lead wolf engaged with Shasta, she would immediately have three wolves attacking her and each from a different angle.

The lead wolf had not decided whether to make the first move, and understood that regardless of who started the physical part of the fight, he only needed to survive the first blows. Once the fight was joined, the other two wolves would attack and from the rear. Once all three wolves were involved, the odds would change in their favour. Ideally, their combined efforts would intimidate the mother bear and drive her and the cubs away. Or, they might disable or even kill the mother bear quickly, perhaps after first blinding her, and then they could chase down and kill the cubs. If the fight was prolonged and not decisive, perhaps they might kill a cub and retreat, but have more than elk meat to return to.

Shasta understood this strategy as well, only she planned a different outcome. Her plan was to quickly kill the lead wolf. A well-placed head or

Third Year — More Experience

upper body swipe, with the full weight of her body thrown into the swing of her paw and with sharp claws extended, would likely be decisive.

Shasta waited until the attention of the lead wolf was focused on the cubs and then she charged uphill faster than the wolf likely imagined was possible. She closed the gap. The wolf turned back and then moved to the side, perhaps thinking to outflank the bear again. However, Shasta had learned and anticipated this. She correctly decided in which direction the wolf would turn. The wolf completed the turn, dug his hind legs into the snowy ground, and then in the last instant before contact, surged forward towards Shasta's head and chest, jaws open and claws extended.

Her first blow was well timed and the head of the wolf ripped apart. Shasta made the swipe with her right paw and the force of the swing carried her full circle. Her eyes momentarily locked with those of Koda and Kodiak as the arc of her gaze passed the cubs.

The eye contact was like an immediate call to arms, and the cubs started to run down the hill before Shasta completed the circle to face the two remaining wolves.

Shasta completed the turn and faced the two wolves. Whether it was due to the sight of the head of their alpha male almost severed at the neck, blood spurting into the sky, or the menacing look of Shasta's eyes locked on theirs, the wolves scattered and ran at break-neck speed, never looking back.

The victory was good, but the bleeding from Shasta's face, neck, and chest confirmed that the fight had not been that lopsided. The wolf had targeted the eyes, but managed to claw only from the face down to the upper chest before Shasta's paw and claws struck. The bleeding was a concern, and Shasta stopped to cleanse the wounds. Kodiak helped with his tongue. Koda, meanwhile, found the roots of the same plant Shasta had used to make the salve for her and Kodiak's wounds. She brought the roots to her mother, who was very pleased.

They stayed in the area for the better part of a week while they finished the remains of the elk and the wolf. Shasta allowed the coyotes to eat at the carcass while they were in the day dens. The black birds and smaller animals also visited the carcasses. There was food for many animals and Shasta did not begrudge them a share of the bounty. However, whenever she or the cubs came into view, the other animals promptly scattered, which is correct, because deference is required when in the presence of a grizzly. The wolves never returned. Shasta and her cubs left the area satiated.

The spring continued dry, and Shasta was thankful for the elk and the wolf since this would be another poor berry year. The cubs were bigger than she had hoped they might be. Kodiak still seemed destined to be a large grizzly, perhaps even larger than his father or grandfather, but his hip injury had slowed him down. So long as there was lots of food, Shasta hoped he might still be one of the great grizzlies, albeit one with a limp.

The third summer is sometimes the last that a cub stays with the mother, and Shasta understood this. Even so, she felt it more likely that the cubs would leave the following year. This seemed best to Shasta, because there was still time over the summer and fall, and even the following spring, for the cubs to learn more before they started their own journeys, and both cubs needed time to recover from their injuries.

Everywhere they went, Shasta was reminded of the dryness. There had not been much rain. Dust flew up from their feet when they walked in the dry meadows and along the animal trails. The mud in the creek beds and sand bars hardened and cracked.

Nature is a wonderful teacher, but also a tough taskmistress. A dry summer and the lightning from a late day thunderstorm provided the opportunity for fire, one of the most dreaded calamities in the forest.

Shasta understood the potential for the threat because she had experienced the aftermath of a fire as a cub with her mother. The prevalent memory from that time was feeding on the remains of animals consumed in the conflagration. As such, Shasta's first thought when she smelled the smoke was of food, but this time, there was something different and ominous about the smell. It grew quickly, and the already warm summer air heated up uncomfortably. Birds appeared overhead and flew fast and furiously away from the smoke. Then, a deer family emerged from the forest from the direction of the smoke. Deer rarely revealed their presence to grizzlies, yet this family took little notice of Shasta or her cubs as they raced pell mell and only a short distance away. The deer did not run in a straight line. They jostled trees and bushes and they sometimes

Third Year — More Experience

bumped into one another. The frantic and frenzied movements high-lighted the fear in their faces.

The sky was hazy at the bottom of the valley and the sun was no longer visible except as a diffuse and faint orange glow through smoke that was now visible and pushed at the forefront of the fire. Shasta understood at once that on this occasion the smoke was their enemy and that without an expeditious escape, they would be trapped in the fire that pursued the deer and the birds.

Running uphill in a valley is hard work, but the body of a grizzly is well suited for this purpose. Their front feet are adapted to digging, and the bears dug in to the valley floor as they ran uphill and then used their huge and powerful hind legs to propel them forward in one massive bound after another. As fast as they were, they were slow compared to the deer that continued to pass them as if they were standing still. Coyotes and wolves joined the retreat, and soon the valley seemed filled with inhabit-ants that otherwise rarely saw each other. Lynx and weasels, marmots and rabbits, squirrels and chipmunks, and mice and voles all scurried as fast as their legs and strength could carry them.

Shasta felt strong and the cubs so far looked fine running behind her. She did not run full speed because she was still faster than the cubs, even without their injuries. Even so, when they started the race from the fire, both cubs kept up well with Shasta. She monitored their speed and discomfort. She did not want to outrun her cubs, and worried that their injuries might cause them to wear out.

Blustery summer winds propelled the fire faster than they could run, and finally a fog of smoke enveloped them and their eyes burned and watered. The temperature of the air increased and they coughed and wheezed as they ran. In due course, the orange flames of fire were visible through the smoke. Shasta heard the cries of the smaller animals that could not escape the flames. Only the larger animals with a longer stride stood a chance.

Shasta understood that their only hope was to climb past the tree line, and above that, in the lee of the mountain, to the higher lake that even in summer was surrounded by snow. Snow and water meant safety. Trees meant death.

The distance seemed daunting, but she felt a confidence that might not have been deserved. Once the flames were visible, the energy of the cubs redoubled and they seemed to fly up the hill. From somewhere inside, the fear engendered a boost of energy. Their lighter bodies were an advantage compared to Shasta. The cubs passed her and increased the gap between them and the fire, and this was the source of her confidence. She felt that as long as she was between the cubs and this enemy, surely they would be fine.

The flames caught up with Shasta and the cubs. Shasta could hear the cracking and popping as the branches of the trees and the dry brush succumbed to the fire. For a while, the fire and the bears ran side-by-side up the valley. Shasta was frightened once the flames were parallel to her, and she positioned herself beside and between the cubs and the fire. The flames gained on the bears, but never overtook them; the winds and the terrain directed the fire to the opposite side of the slope. Shasta had chosen their route well. She and her cubs were on the safer side, and whether this happened by instinct or luck, she neither knew nor cared; she was glad all the same.

The cubs sensed the urgency was past, but Shasta insisted they continue the race to the absolute safety of the water and snow.

Once the lake was in sight, the cubs slowed to a walk, and both limped slowly and painfully to the water. They were parched and dehydrated, and the saliva in their mouths was thick and sticky. Even so, they were too exhausted at first even to drink. Rest needed to come before thirst. Grey ash covered their fur and they looked like ghost bears. When they finally reached the lakeside, they collapsed on the ground.

Shasta noted that both cubs grimaced when they lay down. Kodiak collapsed on his left side but even with this protective manoeuvre, he winced. In a similar fashion, Koda collapsed on her right side, but her left shoulder felt the force transmitted across her back.

Shasta was the first to drink and after slaking her thirst, she splashed water on the cubs and encouraged them to the lakeside to rehydrate. She groomed their fur while they drank.

Looking around, Shasta saw the lake had become a haven for many animals. All were spent, and the usual fear in the presence of natural

Third Year — More Experience

enemies was somehow lost in the luxuriousness of their freedom from the fire. The forest creatures around the lake that afternoon shared the strong bond of survival and for a time they were an unlikely community of adversaries that, if not friendly, was at least accepting.

Shasta and her cubs were the dominant species by the lake, and unless another bear found haven here, they were safe. Shasta did not smell another bear, but before they settled into a day den, she scouted the lake carefully and she chose a den site that afforded a good smell of any animal that might approach the lake. Who knows what animals might be attracted to the carrion left in the wake of the fire?

By dawn the next morning, the sky was clearer, but the smell of smoke lingered. Most other animals had dispersed overnight. As their strength returned, the natural enmities emerged and the fellowship of the lake dissipated like the smoke. The lake seemed quiet when Shasta and her cubs started back down to browse the remains of the animals caught and cooked in the conflagration. They ate their fill of many unfortunate and slower animals and the variety afforded Shasta the opportunity to teach the cubs to choose the best organs when food is plentiful. The fire also made it easier to identify good digging sites for the partially cooked tubers of the creamy-yellow flowers they preferred.[d]

The smell of smoke persisted for many days, the sky stayed intermittently hazy, and the sun had an eerie orange glow, until one day they awakened to the pristine chill smell of mountain air in the morning, a clear sky, and a hot yellow sun. The winds had changed overnight, and the smoke had blown away.

The summer continued dry, and autumn arrived with a poor berry crop, but Shasta and the cubs had enjoyed a meat-filled spring and summer, and digging for roots, tubers, corms, bulbs, ant larvae, and the occasional pine nut cache sustained them well. Shasta was pleased to see that the cubs independently initiated the food forays. Last summer, they had mostly followed Shasta's lead and ate what she found. This year, Koda and Kodiak automatically searched for and dug out pine nut stashes, ant larvae, and the underground plant food.

As the autumn progressed, Shasta was happy and satisfied. Notwithstanding their respective injuries, both cubs were stronger and more resourceful. They had learned well. Kodiak was now three quarters of the size of his mother and Koda over half. The cubs had a good chance of survival, even if they left now.

Higher up in the mountain, past the tree line, and higher still than the alpine lake that had served as the haven from the fire, there was another lake that Shasta knew about. The meadows around the lake were home to marmots and ground squirrels and before the winter came, she planned to visit. There were fish in the lake that might be catchable.

When they reached it, the roar of the waterfall jogged Shasta's memory of her first visit. She had found the lake in the autumn of the year she mated with Ursus. She had gone higher in the mountain to look for marmot dens, which provided the fat stores necessary for her pregnancy hibernation. She'd fed well, and her memories of that first visit were strong and positive. In the intervening three years, she hoped the marmot population had rebounded from her culling.

The cubs had never seen a high waterfall before. The water cascaded over a rocky prominence. Larger rocks at the edge separated the water into many tiny waterfalls that coalesced and separated several times during their journey to the bottom. At the bottom, the waterfall formed a tiny turbulent pool that could not restrain the frothing water for long before it poured into a smooth narrow chute that opened into a larger gorge before finally emerging into the lake.

Fish were plentiful. There seemed to be more now than Shasta remembered. The lake was deep enough for the cubs to practice their swimming, and they bathed and swam in the shallower areas. Kodiak was no longer a mischievous cub with a penchant for trouble. He was more cautious now and treated everything new with respect. Koda no longer needed to watch out for her brother.

The waterfall proved to be a fun shower for the cubs. The hot summer turned into a scorching autumn and between fishing forays and marmot digs, the bears showered under the waterfall to cool off.

When Shasta led them back down from the lake, the marmot and fish populations were less for their visit, and the bears were nutritionally ready for hibernation.

Third Year — More Experience

Shasta found the den unspoiled. The cubs had grown enough that she needed to expand it to accommodate them comfortably and both cubs automatically helped with this process. Shasta realized that this would be her last hibernation in this den, even if the cubs decided to stay for another winter. There was no practical way to expand the den further.

She also understood the cubs were unlikely to stay past the next summer. They were both strong and would likely do well. Kodiak's limp would always be a concern, but given his size, so long as he was thoughtful and deliberate about his actions, he might still take over from his father. Koda's weakness in her left shoulder was also a concern, but otherwise she was certainly larger and stronger than Shasta had been when she was the same age.

Yes, she thought, they will leave next year. She wondered how this would be decided, and realized that she didn't know. Remembering back, she and her mother had separated in the early summer of her fourth year. Late one afternoon, she and her brother found themselves together and apart from their mother. They searched for their mother but she was gone. The leaving just happened. Later that summer, she and her brother separated. And this too, just happened.

FOURTH YEAR —

The Leaving

Kodiak woke her up the next spring. He was up and out of the den with the first warm days. Shasta considered his independence a good sign. Kodiak emerged from the den robust and there was no longer much of a limp. Shasta looked critically for several weeks before she finally accepted that the leg had improved so much. Koda's injury had also healed well over the hibernation, and the weakness with digging was no longer common, and was present only when the excavation was intense. Neither injury seemed like a serious liability any longer, but even so, Shasta worried that someday these old wounds might haunt her cubs and place them at a critical disadvantage.

The winter snows were thick and the spring was wet and lush, which pleased Shasta. This meant lots of food for what would likely turn out to be their last year together. Better to leave when the leaving is good, she thought.

The days were warm and the higher trails muddy and slippery. Soon after they emerged from the den, they found themselves further down in the valley than Shasta had ever taken the cubs before. The lower valley was more dangerous because the area included a corridor used by other bears, and because men sometimes came to this part of the mountains.

Shasta no longer had to find food for the cubs. They had not suckled last year apart from soothing Kodiak after his injury. Since she no longer had to feed the cubs, her energy level was higher, and she emerged from the den feeling as strong as the year she mated with Ursus.

The family browsed in a loose group and always came back to an established day den during the heat of the day. At night, Kodiak foraged, often on his own, and sometimes with his sister. They found a deer carcass and brought Shasta to the location. The southern slopes were filled with tubers and bulbs. Pine nut caches seemed to be everywhere.

Life was good. Almost too easy, thought Shasta. As the days passed with so much food, and so little trouble, the bears relaxed and their natural wariness seemed to subside. Shasta noticed this first in the cubs, but recognized that she also felt carefree, and this worried her.

The next morning, she decided to lead the cubs back up the mountain, but before they could leave, the silence of the morning was broken by a sound that was familiar to Shasta, but strange to the cubs.

Shasta and the cubs sought the safety of the forest and were just in time to escape being spotted by two men in a noisy den that flew in the sky. Although she did not know for sure, Shasta presumed they were looking for bears, and she knew they were dangerous. When man is present, the grizzly is no longer the dominant species.

The flying den settled to the ground and men emerged. In short order they confirmed the presence of the bears. Shasta, Kodiak, and Koda had all rubbed and scratched evergreen trees to sharpen their claws and moult their fur, and the abundance of food resulted in lots of bear scat. Based on the size of the tracks and the height of the scratch marks on the trees, the men estimated that the cubs were perhaps in their fifth spring. Knowing Kodiak and Koda were as big as cubs a year older would have pleased Shasta.

Although Shasta had no way of knowing, the presence of a family with cubs ready to leave was a big plus for the men. If they could collar all three bears, they would be able to study the dispersal of this family unit. They would know where the mother went and if she mated with a collared male grizzly, they would learn the identity of the male and they would then know the genetic heritage of the future cubs. They would

Fourth Year — The Leaving

learn where the cubs travelled to establish their own home ranges. Yes, finding this family was exciting, especially so soon after hibernation. The men were especially motivated to find and collar the bears. They spent only enough time for their preliminary measurements before they took to the air to look for them.

Shasta led the cubs through the forest on animal trails she knew well. Whenever a meadow opened up, she purposefully led them around the clearing and within the protection of the forest canopy. Bushwhacking through a forest where there is no trail makes for slow progress, and, by the end of the day, the bears had not traveled far at all. The sound of the flying den had been intermittently present over the entire day, and several times the men were visible through breaks in the trees. This worried Shasta, who understood that if she could see the men, she and her cubs might be visible to them. The den she selected that night was so deep in the forest that the night sky was barely visible.

The sound of the flying den awakened the bears at dawn. Shasta wondered about staying in the depth of the forest and waiting for the men to give up their search. Waiting, however, seemed indecisive. Her first and strongest instinct was to put distance between the cubs and the men.

Every time the noise of the flying den came near, Shasta felt fear and her cubs picked up and emulated this emotion. The noise of the flying den became a trigger for anxiety. Shasta felt the nervous speed of her heart, and she could see the cubs' distress. Koda shook in fashion similar, but less intensely, to what Shasta observed in the immediate aftermath of the cougar attack. Kodiak responded with aggressive postures.

Shasta no longer felt confident in their ability to escape. On the prior day, the noise of the flying den was much less frequent. Today, the noise was incessant as the men criss-crossed the rising valley.

A strong emotion like fear can lead to mistakes, and bears are not immune. While bushwhacking around yet another meadow, the flying den came close and Kodiak impulsively bolted towards the clearing. Shasta lunged to intercept him, but in so doing, exposed herself on the edge of the clearing at exactly the wrong moment. Although she hustled Kodiak back into the forest, and even though all were now well hidden, the damage was done. The men spotted them, and the flying den hovered over the clearing and taunted the bears to reveal themselves.

Kodiak was all bravado, and Shasta had a difficult time keeping him in the forest. Now an adolescent grizzly male, perhaps he felt invincible. Shasta knew otherwise.

Kodiak had reached an age when he must have felt that making decisions was up to him and that the advice of his mother was discretionary. Shasta offered many strong woofs and growls to keep him in the forest, but Kodiak would have none of it, and eventually he bolted again for the clearing to confront the flying den.

Shasta watched helplessly as her boy cub galloped towards danger. Kodiak only managed to run a short distance before he felt pain in his hip. He turned to look at what felt like a bite from a large and aggressive insect.

Shasta saw his run slow to a walk, and then the walk falter, and finally he stumbled over nothing and fell limp to the ground. Shasta ran to her big boy cub and Koda followed. She grabbed Kodiak with her teeth at the scruff of his neck and dragged him back towards the forest. Koda pulled on a hind leg with her teeth. The suddenness of the rescue caught the men by surprise, and before they could similarly disable Shasta, Kodiak was safe and hidden within the forest.

Shasta expected the men to attack again. The flying den continued to hover for some time but then left.

Shasta understood that Kodiak was still alive because he was breathing slowly and effortlessly. He looked more asleep than hurt.

The quandary was what to do next. Should they wait for Kodiak to wake up? Would he wake up? Should Shasta save Koda and leave Kodiak to the men who would surely return? Should she wait and attack the men when they did return? There was no good answer to these questions, and Shasta decided to stay and protect her boy cub.

Kodiak did not awaken until much later in the day. During their vigil, the flying den returned many times and each return engendered anxiety. The noisy visits of the flying den disappeared with the daylight and Shasta's relief was enormous. By the time the moon was high in the sky, Kodiak was fully awake and he seemed none the worse for the incident.

Fourth Year — The Leaving

His male grizzly ego might have suffered, but Shasta presumed he would let his aggressive nature get him into trouble again if the men came back. As such, she led the cubs on a hard, fast, and direct trip up the valley that night and by morning, the men were a great distance away.

They continued to travel by night until finally, several days after the last sight or sound of the men, the bears reached the high pass where Shasta had taken down the two elk and where Kodiak had been injured. The elk herd had continued to migrate through the pass, but there was no evidence they had visited this year, and Shasta decided to stay in the area in hope that perhaps Kodiak or Koda might learn to take down a yearling elk. This was not to be, but the pass otherwise provided well for food and as they browsed in peace, the bears eventually stopped thinking about the men.

Now feeling safe and looking back to the escape, Shasta was pleased about the encounter with men. Her cubs now understood what it felt like to be stalked by a more dominant animal. By comparison, the cougar stalk was something much less. Her cubs now understood that this two-legged animal deserved great respect. Knowledge and respect are not the same as fear. Shasta definitely felt the fear of man. The men had arrived in a flying den that could travel much faster than a bear, had successfully stalked the bears, notwithstanding Shasta's best efforts at deception, and then when the opportunity presented, had injured Kodiak from a great distance. Yes, thought Shasta, man is an animal to fear. She presumed Koda had also learned this fear, but she was not certain that Kodiak understood this emotion at all, which seemed strange to Shasta. Shasta wondered how Ursus might have reacted, and decided that male bears might well be different.

Shasta and the cubs enjoyed the spring. As the snow receded, they dug up the corms of a graceful yellow flower that appeared within days of the melt.[¹] When viewed from below the snow line, the yellow flowers contrasted starkly with the white edge of melting snow.

Snow gave way to rain and the showers came often. Soon the forest trails were lush with flowers and moss. The air felt thick with moisture and the cubs' fur glistened with a rich velvety texture. Mushrooms were plentiful, and Shasta taught the cubs how to choose the safe varieties.

101

Summer approached and the usual food sources proved better than usual. This year the cubs mostly foraged away from Shasta, sometimes together and sometimes apart, at first for half a day, and then eventually for most of the day. By some mutual understanding, they always congregated back at the day den.

One morning, the bears awakened to find the air very crisp. After stretching her muscles awake, Shasta walked from the day den to the edge of a clearing. There was no wind and the ground in the clearing was covered in tiny ice crystals. Her breaths puffed clouds of moisture into the crisp air. Her paws crunched as she stepped through the grass. Koda followed and then Kodiak. The air warmed up, the ice crystals melted, and the bears dispersed. Koda dug up pine nuts. Kodiak browsed a field of tiny white and pink flowers.[u] Shasta climbed high up the slope and looked for early summer berries.

Later in the morning, Koda joined Kodiak and they went in the direction of their mother, in the hope that she knew best were to find the spring berries to satisfy their adolescent appetite for sweet treats. Their thinking was rewarded. Shasta was in the middle of a meadow of intoxicating low-lying red berries.[b]

As summer approached, the cubs did not seem as though they were thinking about leaving. They still browsed, foraged, and played together, and they always slept together as a content family unit, but during each passing spring day, they spent more and more time separately.

In the mornings, before they went on their separate ways, and sometimes also in the evenings when the cubs were with her, Shasta spent happy hours sitting on her haunches and watching her cubs. She felt the contentment of a job well done. She had nurtured two cubs to adolescence, and within a few years, both would be established in their own home ranges.

Shasta's contentment lasted for many days until summer was established, and this was a glorious time.

Then one morning, from this bliss emerged a new feeling, a stirring. Shasta watched Kodiak, now almost as big as his mother, and she decided that he was a lot like his father. Shasta glanced over at Koda, and she saw herself in her daughter. Shasta began to think of herself with Ursus. The

Fourth Year — The Leaving

stirring grew into a frisson of yearning, and these emotions grew stronger with these thoughts. Over that morning, she developed an irresistible urge to find Ursus, and that day, it just happened.

About this book

For several years during the first decade of the new millennium, I had a home in the foothills of the Rocky Mountains, very close to Kananaskis Provincial Park. During this period, I spent about half my time each month living there and the other time living in the United States, where I worked at the University of Oklahoma. I commuted back and forth. While in Canada, I hiked in Kananaskis about every second day, rain or shine. Over an eighteen-month period, I kept a journal and the records show that I hiked about 45% of the days that I was in Canada. I got to know the Kananaskis trails and wildlife very well.

During these years, I came across approximately 25% of the grizzly bears in Kananaskis Provincial Park. This sounds like a large number, but at that time, the Kananaskis wildlife management specialists estimated that there were only about 25 to 35 grizzlies in the area. As in every region in Alberta, the bear population was in decline.

Bears have always fascinated me. I grew up in Calgary in a generation when bears were commonly habituated to humans. Most boyhood trips to Banff involved a bear encounter, because they freeloaded off tourists on the TransCanada Highway in Banff National Park. The bears had free access to the garbage dumps in the town sites, and, as an adolescent, I watched while they communally browsed the garbage. Habituated bears can become a problem, and both the human and bear populations

105

suffered from this close contact. Modern bear management strategies were introduced, and this helped both species, but tourist development continues to encroach on the traditional home ranges of many grizzlies and the bear population continues to fall in Alberta. A recent report suggests there are only about 700 bears left in Alberta, and the data ominously predicts that without a change in management, they will be extinct in the province sometime after 2050. Ouch!

Shasta and Her Cubs — The Struggle for Survival evolved naturally from those years hiking in Kananaskis. I have always been a keen student of nature and I voraciously read every book on bears that I could find, the most pertinent of which are referenced at the end of the novella. I discovered Ursus, the journal of the International Bear Management and Behaviour Society, and I subscribed to this excellent academic resource. Pertinent articles from this journal are also included in the references.

I am a paediatrician and Shasta started as a book for elementary school-aged children but evolved into a book for a more mature nature enthusiast. I wanted to write a book that explained bear behaviour in a story format. I hoped to de-mystify the grizzly and to help explain something about this species' struggle for survival.

There is much more to be learned, and hopefully a solution will be found to preserve this remarkable species in Alberta.

I have taken liberties with bear behaviour to tell this story. Shasta has the voice of a human mother. As a paediatrician with over forty years of experience, I have a solid understanding of mothers. Shasta's human voice is introspective and philosophical, and grizzly bears are unlikely to have these frontal lobe attributes. However, this liberty allowed for the story format and conveys much more information on true bear behaviour than I could otherwise accomplish.

Grizzly bear populations in North America are found in Alaska, Yukon, British Columbia, Alberta, Montana, and Wyoming. The bears on the Pacific Coast are much larger courtesy of the availability of better food resources, notably the salmon. The information in *Shasta and Her Cubs — Struggle for Survival* includes data predominantly from studies of the grizzly bears in the Eastern Slopes of the Rocky Mountains from Yukon in the north, south through Alberta, to Montana, and finally to

About this book

Wyoming. This is now the southernmost range of a species that historically ranged all the way to Mexico, and which, until early in the last century, ranged into the southwestern United States!

The story starts with the birth of the three cubs and ends when the cubs leave in the fourth summer. Shasta has memories that are interspersed throughout the book and this allows the reader to learn more about adult grizzly bear behaviour and includes information on adult male grizzly bear behaviour, home ranges, denning behaviour, courtship, and mating. Bears must have memories, but not likely similar to those expressed by Shasta.

Shasta does not know the human names for the various plants, insects, and birds that she sees, but she describes the various species sufficiently for identification, and the glossary includes the common and scientific names, and a brief description. Shasta does use the names for the common mammals. The common trees in the region include varieties of spruce and pine, and Shasta does not differentiate the various species of evergreen or of the deciduous trees in the forests.

Bears likely understand the concept of day and night (sunrise and a sunset) and the concept of seasons (changes in temperature, weather, and plant growth), but they do not think in weeks or months, or consider our four seasons. But, for the purpose of this book, Shasta's sense of time is that of a human. Additionally, she and her cubs can see in color, but I am not aware of data to confirm this ability.

Shasta is a protective mother, but in the wild, the care of a grizzly cub is much more casual and this, in part, explains the high mortality rate in cubs.

Shasta leaves her mother a year later than average and she mates and has her first litter one year later than the average for the region. I decided on this timing because the extra year with her mother, and the extra year prior to mating would presumably give Shasta more experience and more growth, which would likely confer an advantage to her cubs. I wanted Shasta to be a more mature and successful first time grizzly mother.

Shasta has three cubs in her first litter, which is higher than average, and her cubs grow faster than the average for the region. I decided on these features, again because I wanted Shasta to do well as a mother, notwithstanding the inherent challenges of the mountain and forest world.

Shasta seeks out her choice of male grizzly to be the father of her cubs, but in the forest world, mating is usually based on a chance encounter during the season when a female is fertile. During this time, a male grizzly is always looking for a female to mate but females are receptive (mating is successful) only when mature enough and between litters. Shasta's romantic sense of mating is not a likely forest scenario. But then, who is to really know?

Basics of Grizzly Bear Behaviour

Grizzly bears on the Pacific coast and on the Eastern Slopes of the Rocky Mountains are the same species,* but their habits and the available food resources modify their behaviours, and especially their size. Data from studies in Alaska and the Yukon show a difference in the average weight of an adult male grizzly to be 357 kg and 145 kg, respectively. Bears on the Eastern Slopes are less than half as heavy, because their food resources are much more limited.[19] Survival for these bears is a greater challenge.

Shasta and her cubs are an Eastern Slopes grizzly family. The information described in this introduction and throughout the novella is based on data predominantly for an Eastern Slopes grizzly. There are differences in food resources and behaviours within this range, but these differences are minor compared to the difference between the Pacific and Eastern Slopes grizzlies. The available food resources, denning behaviour, and length of hibernation vary by latitude.

A grizzly sow is biologically ready to mate by 3.5 years of age,[19] but the mean age of the first litter is 5.9 years.[3] Courtship and mating occurs between mid-May and early July.[19] Pair bonds last for a few hours to a few

----

* More recent DNA typing separates grizzly bears into five different clade lineage groups. Clade III are from Western Alaska, Clade IV from Southern Canada, Montana, and Wyoming, and Clade V from Eastern Alaska and Northern Canada.

weeks. Both males and females are promiscuous and females might have offspring from more than one mate in the same litter. A fertilized egg only implants if the nutritional status of the sow is optimal, which makes great survival sense. Egg implantation occurs in late November, and after a six to eight week gestation, the cubs are delivered.[19] The average number of cubs ranges from 1.7 to 2.3.[19] Cub mortality is high, and up to 26% do not survive the first year. Thereafter, bear mortality continues to be high, with year-by-year attrition, mostly due to human-related causes such as poaching, culling of problem bears, legalized hunting, and motor vehicle- and train-related trauma.

Female bears continue to grow for about nine years and males for 14 years.[19] A full-grown adult male is about 1.5 times the weight of a full grown female.

Den site construction has been well studied and the characteristics described in the book are based on data from the region. A study in Banff National Park revealed that 100% of dens are excavated and 71% are in a forested area. Dens in this region are usually at about 2200 meters and on terrain with a 33% slope.

For male and female grizzly bears in Banff National Park, the average time of entrance to a den is mid-November, and the average time to leave the den is the last week of March.[19] Female grizzlies enter the den earlier and leave the den later than males.

During hibernation, the heart rate and body temperature fall modestly and the bear does not eat or drink or pass stool or urine. All bears lose weight during hibernation. The weight loss of a Yukon grizzly varies from 28-43% during hibernation. The highest weight loss occurs in a pregnant grizzly sow that delivers and suckles her cubs.

Bears are often in a physiological transition state of hibernation in the days immediately prior to entering the den. As well, there is a second stage of hibernation that lasts for 10 to 14 days after the bear emerges from the den. During this period, the bear is active but does not feed or drink the expected amounts and makes little urine. For the purpose of this novella, Shasta and her cubs did not experience these transient hibernation stages, and they were active when they entered the den and immediately active when they left the den.

Basics of Grizzly Bear Behaviour

The home range of a grizzly depends on the availability of food resources and the number of bears in the region. The range of a male is larger than that of a female. For grizzly bears in Kananaskis, the reported range for a male is 1198 km^2 and for a female is 179 km^2 (about 15% of the adult range).

Grizzly bears are omnivores and are opportunistic animals that accept nutrition where and when available. The basic food groups include plants (roots, corms, tubers, stalks, flower, berries), insects (ants, cutworm moths), pine nuts, fish (trout), bird eggs, smaller mammals (ground squirrels, marmots), and larger mammals (killed by accident, by other predators, or by the bear).[6] The predominant food for an Eastern Slopes grizzly is plant based. Evidence for the plant-based diet is based on direct observation and on the laboratory analysis of stomach contents of dead bears or on bear scat and on hair and bone analysis.

Grizzly bears understand the rhythm of plant growth over the spring though autumn months and they seek specific food resources according the life cycle of the plant. There are anecdotal, perhaps mythological, reports of a grizzly bear seeking specific plants for a medicinal value.

The typical rhythm for a grizzly is to leave the den in the spring, to alternate from lower to higher elevations initially to follow the emergence of the spring plant growth and then to follow the emergence of the summer and autumn berries. Early spring finds them in the lower elevations, during later spring they are higher up, then summer finds them in the lower elevations again, and finally they return to the higher elevations and eventually to a den site in autumn. This pattern is likely routinely interrupted based on weather, opportunistic food availability, and the presence of other bears or humans, which have a substantial influence of grizzly behaviour.

Glossary

a) Crow — Corvus brachyrhynchos — The most common black bird in the mountains.

b) Bearberry or Kinnikinnick — Arctostaphylos uva-ursi — Low-lying shrub found in coniferous forests, alpine slopes, and gravel terraces. The drooping pale-pink urn-shaped flowers turn into dull red berries favoured by grizzly bears. The sugar in the berries ferments and produces alcohol.

c) Northern Goshawk — Accipiter gentilis — Found within mixed or coniferous forests, this hawk hunts small birds and mammals.

d) Yellow Hedysarum — Hedysarum sulphurescens — This plant is a grizzly stable and grows in dense clumps along stream banks, in moist woods, and occasionally in the alpine regions.

e) Foxtail — refers to a variety of grasses with bushy spikes that resemble the tail of a fox.

f) Western Spring Beauty — Claytonia lanceolata — These early spring flowers grow from small 2 cm underground corms that are favoured by grizzly bears. The white to pink flowers have purple streaks.

113

g) Heart-shaped Arnica — Arnica cordifolia — Found in coniferous forests, these looking bright yellow flowers shine over heart-shaped leaves.

h) Raven — Corvus corax — These black birds are common in mountainous areas and can be distinguished from crows by the larger size, heavier bill, shaggy throat feathers, and the deeper voice.

i) Golden Eagle — Aquila chrysaetos — These raptors hunt from high in the sky often with spectacular dives to the ground. The powerful wings span up to 5.5 feet.

j) Army Cutworm Moths — Euzoa auxilaris — These moths travel to an alpine climate in late June and early July, where they feed at night on the nectar of wild flowers. Seventy-two percent of the body of these moths is fat, which makes these insects a rich nutritional source for grizzly bears.

k) Raspberry — Rubus idaeus — Common along streams and in rocky places from lower elevations to the alpine region.

l) Cow Parsnip — Heracleum lanatum — Tall bushy plant up to 2.5 meters and found in damp meadows, along stream banks, and in poplar forests. The creamy-white flowers sit in umbrella-like clusters above wide 30 cm green leaves. This plant has a pungent aroma.

m) Gray Jay — Perisoreus canadensis — Found in coniferous forests, this gray-coloured bird has a mostly white head and a whitish belly.

n) Mountain Chickadee — Poecile gambeli — Small grayish birds with a black cap and throat. The black cap is interrupted by a white eye-line.

o) Osprey — Pandion haliaetus — These birds hover over lakes or rivers and then plunge feat first into the water. The birds adjust their feet to orient the fish lengthways in an aerodynamic fashion to carry the prey to the nest.

p) Mountain Ash — Sorbus — These trees produce scores of flat, white clusters of flowers that turn into red clusters of solid berries.

Glossary

q) Cedar Waxwings — Bombycilla cedrorum — This bird travels in small flocks and enjoys berries in the autumn months. The yellow-tipped tails are distinctive.

r) Yarrow — Achillea millefolium — This medicinal plant has flat-topped flower heads arranged at the end of a sturdy stalk. The flower is named for Achilles, the hero of the *Iliad*, who used the plant to treat the wounds of his soldiers during the Trojan War.

s) Ruffed Grouse — Bonasa umbellus — Found in mixed woods, the male creates an arch with the tail feathers and beats the tail-feathers rapidly to produce a "drumming" sound that carries well through the forest.

t) Glacial Lily — Erythronium grandiflorum — This alpine flower is found in open timberline forests and alpine meadows and is one of the first harbingers of spring. The flowers a gold and provide vivid contrast to the white edge of the melting snow. The corms are eaten by bears.

u) Clover — Trifolium — This common urban and rural flower grows in disturbed places from lower elevations up to the subalpine forests.

References

1. Beyers, Coralie (Editor). 1980. Man Meets Grizzly. Boston: Houghton Mifflin Company.

2. Blanchard, B. M., Size and growth patterns of the Yellowstone grizzly bear. Int. Conf. Bear Res. and Manage.1996;7:99-107.

3. Craighead, F.C., 1982. Track of the Grizzly. San Francisco: Sierra Club Books.

4. French, S. P., French, M. G., & Knight R. R., Grizzly bear use of army cutworm moths in the Yellowstone ecosystem. Int. Conf. Bear Res. and Manage.1998;9(1):389-399.

5. Grambo, R.L. & Cox, D.J., 2000. Bear — A Celebration of Power and Beauty. San Francisco: Sierra Club Books, Verve Edition.

6. Gunther, K. A., Shoemaker, R. R., et al. Dietary breadth of grizzly bears in the Greater Yellowstone Ecosystem. Ursus. 2014; 25(1):60-72.

7. Hall, S. S. X & Swaisgood, R. R., Maternal care and cub development in the sun bear. Ursus 2009;20(2):143-151.

8. Herrero, Stephen. 1985. Bear Attacks. Piscataway, NJ: Winchester Press.

9. Libal, N. S. et al., Microscale den-site selection of grizzly bears in southwestern Yukon. Ursus 2012;23(2):226-230.

10. Murray, J.A. (Editor), 1992. The Great Bear. Seattle: Alaska Northwest Books.

11. Naughton, D. 2012. The Natural History of Canadian Mammals. Univ of Toronto Press.

12. Pengelly, I. & Hamer, D., Grizzly bear use of pink hedysarum roots following shrubland fire in Banff National Park, Alberta. Ursus 2006;17(2):124-131.

13. Phillips, H. W., Northern Rocky Mountain Wildflowers. Falcon Guide Books. Helena, Montana. 2001.

14. Robbins, C. T., Schwartz, C. C., Gunther, K. A., & Servheen, C. Grizzly Bear Nutrition and Ecology Studies in Yellowstone National Park. Yellowstone Science. 2006;14(3):19-26.

15. Rockwell, David. 1991. Giving Voice to Bear. Toronto: Key Porter Books.

16. Russell, Andy (Introduction). 1987. Great Bear Adventures. Toronto: Key Porter Books.

17. Russell, Andy. 1967. Grizzly Country. Vancouver: Douglas & McIntyre.

18. Russell, Charles, & Enns, Maureen. 2002. Grizzly Heart. Toronto: Random House.

19. Schwartz, C. C., Miller, S. D., & Haroldson, M. A., Grizzly Bear. Pages 556-586 in G. A. Feldhamer, B. C. Thompson, and J. A. Chapman, editors. 2003. Wild Mammals of North America: Biology, Management, and Conservation. Second edition. Johns Hopkins UP, Baltimore, Maryland. USA.

20. Scotter, G. W. & Flygare, H. Wildflowers of the Canadian Rockies. Hurtig Publishers. Edmonton, Alberta. 1986.

References

21. Sibley, D. A. National Audubon Society The Sibley Guide to Birds. Alfred A. Knopf. New York. 2000.

22. Sorensen, O.J., Totsas, M., Solstad, T., & Rigg, R., Predation by a golden eagle on a brown bear cub. Ursus 2008;19(2):190-193.

23. Terres, J.K., 1991. The Audubon Society Encyclopedia of North American Birds. Wings Books, Avenel, New Jersey.

24. Zager, P. & Beech, J., The role of American black bears and brown bears as predators on ungulates in North America. Ursus 2006;17(2):95-108.

About the Author

Dr. Lane Robson is an academic paediatrician who refined his skills in writing by authoring and publishing over six hundred medical articles. He has also published articles on postal history, William Blake, and CS Lewis. He won the Geldert medal for philatelic writing in 2012.

His successful professional non-fiction book *Stop Washing the Sheets* (http://www.stopwashingthesheets.com) aids parents struggling with the problem of bedwetting, and his 2014 fantasy novel *The Prophecy* tells the story of a lost colony of Vikings in the Canadian arctic.

After travelling and practicing medicine all over the world, Dr. Robson has settled back in his hometown of Calgary with his partner Louise.

Printed in Canada